Madeleine

Madeleine

LAST FRENCH CASQUETTE BRIDE IN NEW ORLEANS

WANDA MAUREEN MILLER

atmosphere press

For my first California friend, Doris Flood Ladd. A half century ago, this beautiful, sophisticated New Yorker saw something of value in an Arkansas redneck and opened the doors to publishing my textbooks and first novel.

Part I.
Port de Lorient, France, April 1728

Chapter 1

Madeleine Boucher knew her life was about to change forever. The strikingly lovely seventeen-year-old sat for the first and last time with her mistress, Countess Louise de Mandeville, in the richly appointed de Mandeville carriage parked dockside at Port de Lorient. She saw a group of young women and nuns waiting nearby on the dock to board *les Belles Soeurs*, a large sailing vessel. The fifty-nine other *filles a la casquette* were picked to be wives of the French settlers in the Louisiana colony and were accompanied by the Ursuline nuns. The girls kept close by their *casquettes*, or trunks filled with their dowries supplied by the French government. Most were poor, respectable girls from good families and had traveled by public conveyance, so they kept looking at the impressive carriage nearby and wondered aloud about its two occupants.

Madeleine heard a tall nun with a faint mustache try to quiet them. "Please, *mes enfants*, you have been picked by the Church and King Louis XV to exert a stable influence on our colony. You will soon be wives of the leading French settlers. Act accordingly, *s'il vous plait*." She knew she would be one of those wives and was frozen with fear at the prospect of being married to a stranger in a strange land.

In the carriage, Madeleine's eyes kept returning to her own *casquette* filled with china and linens, furnished by the Company, and more clothes than she had ever owned, given to her by *Madame* de Mandeville. She wore a sensible navy-blue wool traveling dress with a fitted bodice, making her small waist even trimmer. Its severity was softened by spotless white ruffles flowing from the high neckline and elbow-length sleeves. The dark blue and white complemented her pale white skin and thick abundance of straight black hair, worn unpowdered and pulled into a chignon at the back of her head. Its bulk seemed too heavy for her slender neck and back, always held ramrod stiff. Both women wore capes over their shoulders to protect them from the early morning April chill. Madeleine's was a plain navy-blue wool, and the countess's was fur-trimmed and lined wool. She sat stiffly upright with her hands folded in her lap and kept her blue eyes lowered in deference to her mistress.

The countess, sitting across from her in the carriage, made short little frustrated sighs now and then to show her annoyance. Her manicured fingers toyed with the sable trim of her woolen cape. She had not spoken a word to Madeleine all morning.

Seeking relief from the stifling silence, Madeleine looked at the ship that would take her from the familiarity of her past life to a new world. She had no idea what to expect; none of the girls knew whom they would marry. To avoid looking at the countess, she examined the vessel with conflicting emotions. The ship itself was a curious mixture of opposites. It was at the same time a huge, towering enigma in wood, and yet it looked too small to brave the unknowns of a sea voyage to the other side of the world. It was about 180 feet long with its bow and stern higher than the middle. The deck made a long, graceful curve reminding her oddly of the powerful and proud stallions she used to feed on the de Mandeville estate. As with the horses that, when penned, always seemed to be yearning for the open fields, the ship rocked gently to the undulating motions of the harbor waters and seemed to strain against the ropes tying it to the wharf. The ship appeared to be demanding the freedom of the open ocean. Madeleine understood that feeling well and tried to suppress her excitement and dread battling for domination.

Glancing quickly at the older woman, with her powdered hair and elaborate silk dress, Madeleine returned her gaze to the ship with the same fascination she might have shown a snake. Its hull was painted a dark black with red trim along the moldings and rails of the deck, culminating in a small structure of richly carved wood and windows, denoting the captain's cabin at the stern. Her head lowered automatically as her eyes followed the three straight, erect masts as they rose from the deck to tower in the sky, almost tickling the white puffs of morning clouds drifting in from the ocean. Taking a deep breath, Madeleine became aware of exotic odors and sounds: the smell of pitch and salt water, the sounds of the creaking, groaning ship, and the solemn tempo of the crew singing out some sailor's song as they struggled to load the cargo

5

holds.

The older woman finally spoke, "Girl, it is not too late to change your mind and return to your parents' farm."

"*Non, Madame*, I will not go back; there is nothing for me there." Her thoughts raged. She would never go back to that hovel to once again become a serf, like her parents, beaten down and groveling in the dirt for their overlords. She would never again be a servant to anybody. Or let a man dominate her as her father did her passive, quiet mother.

"You must understand I can no longer keep you in my home, even though you are the best lady's maid I ever had. You learn quickly."

"*Oui, Madame*." She was surprised and pleased at her mistress's praise.

"I hope you understand why I must send you away. It is for your own good."

This time Madeline looked away without answering. They both knew why Madeline was being sent away, and it had nothing to do with her best interests.

"In our colony, you will have the opportunity to marry a man of a better class than you would here. There is a shortage of decent women for the colonists. After the last shipments of women from the streets and prisons, our Frenchmen will be grateful to...."

"To marry even someone like me, *Madame*?" Madeleine finished for her.

The mistress looked sharply at her maid but decided to ignore her mocking tone. She felt a twinge of guilt at sending her to a place of such unknown dangers. In spite of herself, she felt responsible for the girl. After all, she had plucked her at age thirteen from her home, the brightest of all the girls on their country property, to be a kitchen maid. Thin, quiet, and obliging, the girl even then showed promise. Who could have guessed that she would turn out to be such a beauty with the dignity of a queen?

Unfortunately, she was also the best servant they had ever had. She seemed to anticipate orders before they were spoken. She learned to cook a better soufflé than their chef. She knew without being told twice which wines complemented which meats. When she was promoted to parlor maid, the house was never cleaner or in better order. All was accomplished with a quiet efficiency.

Occasionally she put a piece of furniture in a different place. At first this amused the countess, that is, until she realized that Madeleine's new arrangements were somehow more fitting or more practical or more symmetrical than her own. When Madeleine was finally promoted to be her own lady's maid, both mistress and maid knew that she was capable of running the whole household even though she was then only sixteen. She had become indispensable. Until now. Oh, well, the countess thought with a sigh, fate is not always obliging. The girl couldn't be blamed for the count's roving eye, but she would be the one to pay.

The countess thought again of the girl's destination. Though there was much dinner table talk of this paradise called Louisiana, where one could get rich quickly, her husband had given her a more realistic picture. After all, as one of the early investors in stock there, he had lost a small fortune in John Law's Mississippi Bubble. She suspected her husband's grim view was partially motivated by his desire to keep Madeleine in his home. Even so, she was alarmed that she had encouraged the girl to go to what the count claimed to be an uncivilized swamp infested with insects, alligators, and wild savages. She worried that Madeleine was going to a place occupied for the most part by criminals and indigents sent there simply to fill quotas for French settlers.

The countess looked at the beautiful, unyielding girl in front of her. Where did she get those thin, aristocratic features? Could she possibly be an *enfant d' amour* of her own father or of the count? The two women could easily be taken for sisters sitting there. *Non*, the girl could not be trusted to stay in her place. If she were merely a good servant, the countess would gladly keep her. Madeleine's quick intelligence and determination showed even now through her fright. It fairly crackled in her snapping blue eyes taking in the scene outside the carriage window.

The Countess de Mandeville remembered that too many times Madeleine had been mistaken for a family member when she was out of uniform. She had more poise and better manners than the countess's own daughter, and she spoke as well as her mistress. She thought of her own unease at the maid always watching her and copying her manners and speech. Madeleine's metamorphosis from ignorant peasant to accomplished lady's maid had been truly remarkable. Somehow she had persuaded her daughter's tutor to teach her to read and write a little. Evidently she could even play the pianoforte by ear. The countess had surprised Madeleine once in the music room, mistakenly thinking it was her daughter who was playing and who had finally profited from her years of music lessons.

The countess could see that her husband was torn between indulging the girl as their protégée and taking her as his mistress. She had to admit, however, that she had never seen Madeleine behave improperly, not even a flirtatious look. Perhaps her cool self-sufficiency and unapproachable manner was a part of her attraction. The girl had to go!

"Did you sew the brooch and the *livres* into the lining of the *casquette* for safekeeping? Remember, the less desperate you look when you get there, the better the marriage you will make."

"*Oui, Madame, merci.*" Madeleine thought with pleasure of the solid gold brooch with the Mandeville crest fashioned in the center. The *livres* represented all the money she had saved in the three years she had worked for the de Mandevilles, plus a small bonus, making a total of 978 *livres*.

The older woman appeased her conscience with the memory that Madeleine had quickly accepted her offer to sponsor her to the Ursuline nuns as a *filles a la casquette*.

Finally, a seaman shouted "All aboard!" and the other *casquette* girls and nuns swayed up the gangway to the ship.

Madeleine turned to Countess de Mandeville, inclined her head slightly, and thanked her, "*Merci, Madame*, for all you have taught me. I will never forget you."

"Nor I you, Madeleine."

Both women were sharply aware of the irony in each other's voices. Madeleine gracefully stepped down from the carriage and joined the other *casquette* girls boarding the vessel for Louisiana.

Michael O'Brien, the red-haired Irish clerk, checked off the women as they climbed aboard the huge merchantman sailing vessel. A tall, commanding man in a braided coat, obviously the captain, stood behind him. Madeleine tried not to look at the captain. Michael's eyes widened as Madeleine took her turn, but he tried to remain businesslike. "And your name, *Mademoiselle*?"

"Madeleine Boucher of the de Mandeville chateau." She could not resist stressing the de Mandeville name; she had seen the other girls gawking at the carriage when she climbed out. She knew she would be the only servant in the group, so she might as well be associated with one of the noblest houses in France. The clerk was so distracted by her beauty, poise, and assurance that he did not hear all her words and repeated, "Madeleine Boucher de Mandeville," mistaking her last name.

Madeleine drew in her breath. She saw the handsome captain's eyes flicker, but she remained silent. She nodded and moved on, her heart pounding at her deception. Should she correct the error? But who would know besides the captain? Would he tell or even care? She had never met the other girls or the nuns. She had been interviewed by Company officials and become a *casquette* girl through the Countess de Mandeville's influence.

With one stroke of the quill, she was elevated from servant to nobility. She set her chin and thought, this a new start. By all that is holy, I can appear to be a lady as well as anyone. She thought of her former mistress's reaction if she knew of her deception, and her ordinarily composed face lit up with a smile, further dazzling the clerk, plus the captain and two crew members standing nearby.

Chapter 2

Following the other girls in the line ahead of her, Madeleine walked along the deck past groups of sailors busy with their tasks, noting with alarm that some of the men leered at the passing group of women. As the girls reached a small hatch in the center of the deck just in front of the mizzenmast, Madeleine became a little dizzy, for the hatch seemed to disappear slowly into the bowels of the ship. She carefully half-stumbled down a steep ladder to a dark passageway, since there seemed to be no ladylike way to descend the ladder.

The contrast between the invigorating ocean air on the deck and the stagnant odors below was staggering. Dimly lit by lanterns on each end, the narrow passageway was formed by two canvas walls stretched the length of the upper hold. They were led into small living spaces with other canvas dividers so that the sixty girls and the nuns were stuffed, five to an enclosure, into the confines of the upper cargo hold. Madeleine, a country girl, got dizzier at the thought of living in these confined quarters for the four or five months of the voyage. The other girls were a great deal more vocal in their complaints.

A ship's officer walked down the passageway, pausing at each enclosure to poke his head through the flap door. He introduced himself as Andre La Boeuff, the captain's mate. Extending the captain's apologies for the modest accommodations, he patiently explained to each group of women that *les Belles Soeurs* was a merchantman built to carry cargo and not to transport passengers. Then he announced that the captain wanted all the passengers on deck in fifteen minutes.

Madeleine shared her compartment with a sweet-faced, quiet nun from the Paris order, Sister Pauline; a petulant, voluptuous blond, Suzanne; and two plain sisters, Delphine and Simone. The ceiling was so low that Madeleine, taller than the others, had to stoop a little to keep from hitting her head on the large beams running across the ceiling. The worst part of all was the odor. Madeleine soon realized from the sounds and smells coming from the deck beneath her feet that their enclosure was located directly over the portion of the lower hold where the livestock was penned to provide fresh meat.

The other girls, especially Suzanne, complained loudly and bitterly about their new home for the next few months. Madeleine, accustomed to poor living conditions and livestock before living with the de Mandevilles, resigned herself and quietly began to put away her belongings. All the women, including Sister Pauline, were a little in awe of her and the de Mandeville name. For the first time in her life, Madeleine was treated automatically with respect without having to earn it. Simone asked her if she would like first choice of bunks. Delphine offered to put away her *casquette*. Suzanne, clearly accustomed to being the center of attention because of her beauty and expensive clothes, appeared a little sullen and pouted.

Mon Dieu, Madeleine thought, what power there is in a name! I will not give this up. She vowed to watch the other girls carefully, and whatever she did not already know about being a lady she would learn on this voyage.

A boy of about twelve scampered down the ladder, his face glowing with the excitement. He was called Jean, he announced, one of the three apprentice midshipmen. It was time for the women to be on deck, he said with glee, then began the process of herding the girls out of their enclosures into the passageway and up the ladder, all struggling to maintain their balance in the dark passageway as the ship seemed to rock in four directions at once.

On the main deck again, Madeleine was grateful for the sunshine and fresh air. She glanced up at the quarterdeck and saw the captain standing with his trim, over-six-foot frame silhouetted against the cloudy morning sky. Delphine put her mouth up to Madeleine's ear. "My, but he's a handsome one with that trim beard."

Madeleine allowed herself a small, amused smile; then she quickly joined the other girls following young Jean up the ladder to the quarterdeck. Pausing at the top rung of the ladder, the boy called out to the captain, "By your leave, sir."

"Granted," the captain responded with barely a look in the boy's direction.

Once on the quarterdeck, the boy herded the group of women to the rear of the deck. "We have to get out of the way," he offered in explanation for packing them into spaces smaller than prison cells.

All over the ship, the activity increased to almost a fever pitch. Small groups of men scurried about in what looked to Madeleine like controlled confusion, but she realized it must be a carefully planned ballet of motions. Each member of the crew moved as a part of the whole unit, more than likely knowing exactly what each of his fellows would do in any given instant in time. The captain silently watched every move his men made with an air of absolute power and control.

Madeleine watched the captain as he stood with his feet spread slightly apart, hands on his hips, as if the energy from his own body were flowing down through his legs to the deck and into each member of the crew. He seemed like such a tyrant in the way he shouted orders and barked reprimands that Madeleine asked Jean, "Is he a horrible man?"

Wheeling to face her, the boy's chest puffed out like on the roosters she used to feed at the estate. "Oh, no... no, *Mademoiselle*. Captain Beauchamp is the finest of men, good and generous to the crew and always considering our welfare above all. There is no better captain who ever sailed any of the seas of the world." Then, with a broad grin no doubt from the pride at finally being of some importance, he took a stance in front of the women clearly in imitation of this man he so admired. "There can be only one captain, one person to make decisions for the common good of all. When the captain is on the quarterdeck, even God Himself must obey him."

The shocked gasp from the nuns jolted him into realizing that his word choice was not the best. He quickly began to stammer a clumsy apology when he was saved by the captain's voice. "You there, boy."

Young Jean's face went rigid with alarm as he wheeled to face the captain, "Aye, sir."

"Since you have taken such an interest in the welfare of the passengers, you are relieved of your normal duties for the remainder of the voyage." The boy's small shoulders sagged in hurt and disappointment, but the captain went on, "I charge you with the very important assignment of seeing to the care and welfare of these ladies during the voyage." Madeline could see the boy's shoulders shoot back with his thin chest puffing out once more. "They are your responsibility, son, and I know you will not fail in your assignment."

"Oh, yes, sir. Thank you, sir. I will do my best, sir." When young Jean turned to face them again, he had a wide grin stretched across his face.

Madeleine shot the captain a quick look of approval for his unexpected sensitivity toward the boy—a look he seemed to notice with a little twitch in the corner of his mouth. He ordered the men to make final preparations for sea. "See that the lines are singled up fore and aft and launch the long boat."

He then turned to the women and formally welcomed them aboard the ship, setting down the rules they were expected to live by on their journey. The women would be divided into four groups and alternate eating their meals in the captain's main cabin with one of the officers. They would be allowed to walk for exercise on the quarterdeck only, always in their assigned group and were to stay away from all common seamen during the voyage.

As he spoke, Madeleine noticed that the captain's

demeanor reminded her of the gentlemanly manners displayed by the aristocratic visitors to the de Mandeville estate. He was definitely a curious enigma of contrasts and surprises. Bowing gracefully, he then left the women, who were murmuring compliments that would have made him blush had he heard them, and turned his attention once more to the ship and the process of getting underway.

As if on cue, the flurry of activity by the crew increased to an almost frenzied pitch. The ship's long boat was lowered into the harbor. As the lines holding the vessel to the wharf were let go, it began to tow the ship out into the main channel, where the current took it gently and began moving them toward the open ocean. Jean was in his glory standing on the rear of the quarterdeck and describing the chain of events to his new charges, as if he were a miniature version of the captain.

For Madeleine, it was a time of both excitement and of sadness as the great sails were lowered from the yards, filled with the wind, and began moving the ship under its own power. As the shores of France grew smaller in the increasing distance, all of the women stood as if paralyzed, watching the receding shoreline. Madeleine had long since made up her mind that the past no longer held anything of value for her, and she found her eyes drawn toward Captain Beauchamp.

Over the next week, the ship's routine settled into a never changing series of activities that became so familiar she could tell the time of day. Young Jean shepherded them about in their groups of fifteen: morning exercise and clean-up on deck, the meals taken in the captain's large port cabin, afternoon exercise, and finally the evening meal. Occasionally they had the treat of an early evening stroll on deck with the cold sea breeze whipping the exposed flesh of faces and hands. Madeleine could enjoy the bounty of stars peppering the night sky. Sometimes she felt suspended in time, as if she were in a dream where the past had long since ceased to exist and there was now only the feeling of a new beginning.

Chapter 3

Captain Jean Paul Beauchamp watched his ship leave the shore and thought about his precious cargo of sixty virtuous young maidens and six nuns. *Mon Dieu*, what a voyage this would be. If anything happened to them, he would never again be allowed to anchor off the Louisiana territory's shores. He thought of the tall, cool beauty, Madeleine de Mandeville, as she called herself. She could be quite a temptation.

He forced himself to think of his new command and of the voyage ahead. It was not an easy trip from France to Louisiana, taking from three to five months, depending on the weather. He knew he was young at thirty to be in command of *les Belles Soeurs*. The two wealthy Parisian merchants who owned her had searched carefully to find a captain to be responsible for their large investment. The ship was prime pickings for the greedy pirates that preyed on ships sailing to the Louisiana colony, for most of them were heavily laden with supplies and materials worth a royal ransom.

Captain Beauchamp, an unusually tall man with broad shoulders and the iron physique of a laborer in the mines, was well prepared to command this rich vessel that the owners, Monsieurs Lebouchet and Dupre, expected to compound their wealth. Captain Beauchamp, the son and grandson of Admirals Rene and Louis Beauchamp respectively, had earned this job through his experience and his daring forays while in command of his Majesty's frigate, the *Challenger*, in spite of his being dismissed.

On the surface, his dismissal was caused by a scandal concerning the mysterious death of his wife that resulted in his leaving the navy in disgrace. But the truth behind his dismissal was actually based on his near legendary exploits. His series of masterful victories over the King's enemies and his unparalleled seamanship destined him to be a powerful candidate for Admiral of the French fleet. This possibility created envy in his senior officers and led to his downfall.

At court his political enemies, aided by jealous admirals, were able to plant in the King's mind the idea that Beauchamp had understated the value of the prizes taken by the *Challenger*, thus reducing the King's share of the booty. To add to the suspicions about him, Beauchamp's prize master disappeared with a large portion of the booty. With Beauchamp's aid, his prize merchant was captured and charged with several crimes against the Crown. It was a simple matter for Beauchamp's enemies to bribe the prize merchant to implicate the famous captain of the *Challenger* and ensure his downfall.

Lebouchet and Dupre, indifferent to court gossip and

intrigue, were delighted at their good fortune in having such a competent captain for the flagship of their merchant fleet. Certainly they would sleep with greater ease knowing *les Belles Soeurs* was in the hands of one of the most experienced fighting men in France.

Beauchamp had inspected his charge with a critical eye. "*Mon Dieu*, a merchantman!" She had none of the graceful lines and spirited responsiveness of his beloved *Challenger*, nor its grandeur and power, but she was a well-built ship and was his to command. Plus, she had guns to protect herself.

The captain's gray eyes reflected his disillusion. He was haunted by the loss of his wife, and he still felt the disappointment of losing his more prestigious command. He accepted that he was a sailor, not a politician. He could not weather the storms of Court and climb the top-mast to an admiral's position, but he had to admit he liked the adventure he had found in shepherding provisions to Louisiana in the New World. As a bonus, he could console himself with the thought of the profits accruing to the master of a merchantman for each successful voyage. After a few years of this, and then with the wealth promised by the venture, he could buy his own ship—something fast and sleek, one of the new ships being built in New England, where daring new designs were the talk of ship owners and seaman alike.

The excitement of this voyage welled up in him and displaced all thoughts of his misfortune as he walked the deck of *les Belles Soeurs*. His first mate, a burly ruffian from Marseilles, came up and pointed out the new bonnets laced to the sails. "*Mon capitaine*, we will be able to make quick work of shortening sails; these bonnets make the lacing spill itself...."

"*Oui*, Andre, you do not need to instruct me in seamanship. We have a much greater problem than worrying about shortening sails. Keeping our crew away from these *casquette* girls may be more trouble than hurricanes and pirates striking at the same time."

Andre's eyes lit up like an ammunition magazine exploding, and his face cracked with a grin wide enough to wrap around a mizzenmast. "Ah, *Capitaine*, a pleasure trip is in store for us."

"Do not even think of pleasure! Any man who touches one of these maidens will be promptly keel-hauled."

Andre thought of this practice of suspending a seaman on a rope from the bow of the ship into the sea, dragging him under the keel, heaving him up and dropping him again. If his mates liked him, they might pull the unfortunate seaman up so fast he would not drown, but that often resulted in his flesh being ripped off by the barnacles. Andre felt his ardor cool immediately.

Chapter 4

A few weeks out, the passengers wished they had never seen *les Belles Soeurs* or the sea. Mountainous clouds had built up overnight, and a fierce storm buffeted the large vessel about like a toy ship. The women, most suffering from severe seasickness, had been confined to their cabins and the lower deck for three days. Many did not care, for they were sure they were going to die. Others, like Madeleine, recovered early and chaffed at the restriction even in their terror. But they feared the captain even more than the storm; he had become a fierce tyrant who would tolerate no disobedience of his orders.

The third night of the storm, Madeleine, unable to bear the stale, close air and the nauseating odor of vomit any longer, sneaked halfway up the ladder to the hatch cover leading to the upper deck. She felt she had to breathe some fresh air. The cold, wet wind whipped the cape about her body. Her hair loosened from its tight bun and blew wildly into her eyes and face. She heard the captain bellowing orders to his crew to shorten the main sails. As her head topped the upper deck, she could barely make out the men on the yards scurrying to grab lines in order to haul in the enormous canvas sails. Other members of the crew desperately held on to tenuous perches on the yardarms as they pulled in the wet sails.

The captain, looking like a bearded demon as a flash of lightning illuminated him, stood fast by the helmsman, who was holding the bow steady to the wind. The ship rose to meet the oncoming Atlantic storm rollers; and, as the ship's bow struck, the heads of the waves sprayed all those on deck, including Madeleine, like a hail of tiny needles. She clutched the rail to avoid being blown back down the stairs.

Suddenly the wind died and the power of the sea abated as the ship entered the eye of the storm. Madeleine recovered her balance enough to climb the last step to the upper deck, only to fall headlong into a hard chest with brass buttons. She gasped as firm hands steadied her on her feet. She was about to scream when she felt a beard tickle her forehead and heard the captain's voice say, "Is that you, Madeleine? Why aren't you below with the others?"

In her confusion, she did not notice he had used her first name. "Because the air down there was too foul to breathe any longer. I simply had to breathe clean air, even if I fell overboard." She was in no mood to be bullied. "This wooden trough you call a ship smells like a floating pigsty."

"It smells of the passengers it carries and nothing else. Now go back below at once. I do not have time to protect you from the wind or the sea, not to mention from my men once they sniff you out."

Madeleine recoiled at his crudeness and shrugged out of his grip, only to fall against the railing as a huge wave drenched the decks. With one hand, Captain Beauchamp grabbed her around the waist to keep her from falling down the ladder; the other he kept on the railing. This time she did not protest. The two of them swayed in the wind taking comfort from each other's warmth. Madeleine, who had never been in a man's arms before, was amazed at how pleasant it was to lean against his hard chest.

"Madeleine," he said gruffly, "why are you on this voyage to that godforsaken Louisiana territory? You are beautiful and clever enough to find a husband in France, even if you are *not* a de Mandeville."

Madeleine stiffened in shock but remained in the protection of his arm. To his surprise, she did not pretend ignorance or indignation but asked with resignation, "How did you know?"

"I seem to recall the boarding clerk mistaking your name on the day we left. I was watching, do you not remember? I looked over the Company's register of names. I have a copy in my cabin. There is no de Mandeville, only a Madeleine Boucher, serf's daughter and servant of the de Mandevilles."

Madeleine paled at his words. She lifted her head and tried to look at him in the darkness. The captain could feel her breath on his chin. If he lowered his head, he thought, he could kiss her. "What do you intend to do, *Monsieur*? What do you want from me? I will not beg you to keep my secret." Nor will I give myself to you, she thought, straining away from his body as much as she could in his tight grip, but he did not let go.

"You silly chit, what do you think I want?" he bellowed. "Do you think I have to blackmail women into my bed? I don't give a damn if you are the Queen of France or a woman of the streets. *Mon Dieu*, I don't blame you for taking advantage of someone else's mistake. That was quick thinking. Our countrymen in Louisiana are as class snobbish as they are in France."

Madeleine relaxed in his arms again, "Then why did you not continue to pretend? Why did you shame me?"

"*Ma petite*, there is no shame in trying to be better than people think you are. The colonies are a good place to make a new start, but the French will forgive any lie except about family. That is sacred. Do you think you can carry it off?"

"*Oui*, I can carry it off. I *must* carry it off. I will never bow and scrape to anyone again." She thought bitterly of her days at the estate.

The captain rumbled a low laugh in his chest, "I do believe you can. At any rate, no one will ever learn your secret from me."

"*Merci*, Captain," Madeleine lifted her head and grazed his cheek with her lips.

The captain's voice grew husky. "Now, *Mademoiselle* de Mandeville, you must go below or I may change my mind about blackmailing you. Unfortunately, I have made a vow to deliver a cargo of sixty virgins and deliver all sixty intact I will."

Madeleine, fleeing his frankness as much as the storm, stroked his cheek with her hand and stumbled down the stairs to the familiar haven of her cabin.

Chapter 5

A few nights after the storm, *les Belles Soeurs* and its inhabitants had returned to normal. Most of the women had recovered from their seasickness and their fright, and the captain and crew were rested from their exertions, or as rested as they could be on a busy ship.

To celebrate, Madeleine, Sister Pauline, Sister Mary, and Suzanne dined at the captain's table. It was the first time during the voyage that the distant-mannered Captain Beauchamp had deigned to invite some of the girls, naturally accompanied by at least two nuns, to dine with him and his first mate, Andre. The women enjoyed the privilege because it was a welcome change from their usual meals. Madeleine and Suzanne were conscious that the other women were looking at them with envy.

The captain had insisted on using a white linen tablecloth set with his own silver plates and on furnishing wine from his private stock. Ordinarily the *casquette* girls and the nuns ate together after the crew had eaten. They had to dine in the same fashion the crew did, often cleaning up after their greasy mess. The good Sisters always insisted on the clean-up, of course. Even though it was hardly elegant dining, the girls had become accustomed to dipping from the same large bowl and sharing the few pewter and wooden plates and utensils.

Sister Pauline exclaimed, "*Mon capitaine*, this is such a treat for us. We all feel so festive after the storm. It is a pity poor Simone and Delphine could not join us as you invited all the girls in our cabin. They are still too weak from the *mal de mer*. We thought Suzanne would not be well enough to join us either. But here she is, pretty as a picture, with blooming cheeks."

Madeleine thought Suzanne's cheeks were blooming rather unnaturally in her pale face. She suspected her of secretly dipping into her rouge pot so she would be allowed to join them. Or perhaps, considering the brazen way she was fluttering her eyelashes at the captain, she had tried to make herself attractive for him. Certainly her décolletage was low enough to catch his eye. The first mate could not keep his eyes from Suzanne's ample bosom, accentuated by her red brocade dress. The elongated, ornamental panel covering her waist made her look particularly ripe for a girl her age.

Captain Beauchamp interrupted Madeleine's thoughts with assurances to the nun, "It is my pleasure. You all weathered the storm quite well, especially *Mademoiselle* de Mandeville; one would never take her for a landlubber." He turned his intense gray gaze on Madeleine. Wearing a simple white wool dress with seed-pearl buttons her only decoration, she provided a contrast to the flamboyant

Suzanne. Only Madeleine's white neck showed above her simple ruffled collar.

Feeling his eyes on her, Madeleine took a sudden interest in her plate. "I was luckier than the others, *Monsieur*, to recover so quickly."

The captain and Madeleine were lost in their own thoughts for a moment, letting the conversation of the others drift by them. They were both remembering the third night of the storm and their encounter on the upper deck. Their reverie was broken by Sister Mary's remark directed to them about the food. "Madeleine, you are not eating your food. You must keep up your strength; you are badly needed by us all. Captain, it is wonderful to have fresh mutton again. I really did not expect fresh meat on our voyage."

"I am happy that you like it. Enjoy it while you can. So many of our live animals were washed overboard during the storm and drowned and so few recovered that we must eat as much of their meat as we can before it spoils. I'm afraid it will be feast now, famine later. We will run out of live animals in a couple of months and be forced to eat only salted meat."

Suzanne leaned toward him, dangerously increasing her décolletage. "Captain, you are *tres* clever to think of live animals aboard ship just to feed us well." She gave him a teasing look. "We have almost become accustomed to their odor."

"*Merci, Mademoiselle*, but the idea did not originate with me. Also, it did occur to me that my crew would benefit from having decent food."

Suzanne pouted prettily at his rebuff.

Sister Pauline tried to turn the conversation in a more

harmless direction. "Perhaps by the time we run out of fresh meat we may be able to supplement our meals with the vegetables we are growing on deck. Another excellent idea of yours, Captain."

"You ladies have been taking good care of them. You showed good sense in taking them below during the storm to keep them from being blown away."

Sister Pauline looked fondly at Madeleine, still silent. "That was Madeleine's idea. As a matter of fact, she has done most of the work in caring for the vegetables. She has quite an instinct for growing them."

Suzanne added, "*Oui*, she is quite the little farmer. One would think she was born to it."

Madeleine, avoiding the captain's eyes, coolly defended herself, "In a way, I *was* born to it. I lived the earlier part of my life on the de Mandeville country estate. When the other de Mandevilles were in Paris, I frequently helped oversee the cultivation of the gardens, including the vegetable gardens. I like to make myself useful."

"How boring to be useful," Suzanne responded. "I prefer to be decorative."

The captain noted wryly, "Unless you marry a very wealthy man with numerous slaves, you may go hungry as a mere decoration."

Sister Pauline objected, "*Mais*, surely not, *Monsieur*. I thought food was plentiful in Louisiana."

Andre snorted at this. The captain gave him a silencing look. "It is when you can find someone who will grow it. I am afraid the French landowners cannot find enough people to work the land. Both they and the soldiers are more interested in gambling, drinking, and other *les plaisirs de la nuit* than they are in working."

Madeleine asked, "I thought John Law, Director of the Company, has been sending common people to settle the colony."

The captain was surprised at her being so well informed. "That is true; he did indeed send some very common people—convicted murderers, thieves, salt smugglers. Then he sent a convoy of female convicts to be their wives—drunkards and blasphemers at best and murderers, prostitutes, and knife experts at worst. Most of these women were branded on the shoulders with the *fleur de lis*."

The women looked at each other in shock. Captain Beauchamp continued, "His intent was good, but he could not get decent people to emigrate. So he got settlers any way he could—even kidnapping some, I hear. He had to get immigrants to keep up the stock in the company."

Madeleine mused, "How ironic that the stock collapsed anyway."

Andre returned to the subject of the settlers, "These scum are too lazy to do a day's work. Even if they were willing, they are city scum. They know nothing about growing food."

The captain tried to reassure the women, "I don't want to alarm you, ladies, but it is better to know the problems you face. Actually, the food shortage is not as bad as it used to be. When the colony depended entirely on supplies sent from France, the Company forgot to send enough supplies for the increasing number of immigrants. Quite a few settlers, expecting to get rich on gold or silver, starved to death. The shipments of Negroes to work as slaves have improved matters. But the biggest contribution to New Orleans's food supply is from the Germans."

The Germans? *Pourquoi?*" Sister Mary questioned.

"*Oui,* John Law's Germans, peasants who emigrated to his own land grant on the Arkansas River. When the stock in the Louisiana colony went down and his Mississippi Bubble, as it was called, burst, he had to abandon his land grant. His German settlers came to *La Nouvelle Orleans* looking for passage back to Europe."

"How unfortunate," Sister Pauline said. "Did they get passage?"

"*Non,* luckily for New Orleans. They were given small land grants twenty miles north of the city. It is now known as *Cotes des Allemande,* or the German Coast. Their farming knowledge and hard work, combined with Louisiana's fertile land is feeding most of New Orleans."

Madeleine seemed relieved, "So it *is* possible to grow food in Louisiana."

"*Oui,* I am no farmer, but even I can see that the climate and soil are perfect for cultivation. I predict that agriculture is Louisiana's future, not mining as the Company thought."

Madeleine appeared struck by the thought of her new homeland as one made up of farmers. "That is *tres interesante, Monsieur.*"

The captain continued on a more positive note, "At least now the Company tries to combine its interests with those of the settlers. It is finally distributing slaves to landowners who will grow tobacco, as the Company needs tobacco. It is amazing how many people started growing tobacco. You will find it growing in small back yards right in New Orleans."

The women laughed obligingly, except for Madeleine. "You do not think highly of our countrymen, *Monsieur.*"

"On the contrary, *Mademoiselle*, I admire their ability to enjoy themselves. But you will have to admit that the British colonies have grown much more rapidly because of their piety and industrious natures. I will venture another prediction: that France will eventually lose all her colonies in North America to the British or the Spanish. Or perhaps the colonies will band together and choose to govern themselves."

They all laughed at his wit.

Madeleine put up a small defense of France. "You have to admit that the French Huguenots who have settled in have been extremely successful."

Sister Mary objected, "I hardly think these heretics are an appropriate example to prove your point."

Captain Beauchamp laughed, "Besides, they are more like the British in temperament and religion. They will blend with the British. In New Orleans, people from other countries blend with the French. That is the secret of the city's charm."

Andre too offered a defense of the French. "You can't blame a man for not wanting to work in that damned wet heat and cold—*pardonez moi, Mesdames.*"

The captain agreed with him, "It is true. The place would try the hardiest of souls."

Encouraged, Andre went on, "If the weather doesn't get you, the bugs or the Indians will."

The captain shot him a warning look as the women cried out in alarm. Suzanne grasped the captain's arm and clutched it to her chest. He gently loosened his arm, giving her hand a little pat, and tried to reassure them. "Don't alarm yourselves. New Orleans is in no immediate danger. It is protected by French troops."

Sister Mary questioned him, "But there *is* danger?"

Captain Beauchamp reluctantly replied, "There are some problems with the Chickasaw and Natchez Indians, mostly outside New Orleans."

Madeleine too pressed him for answers, "I insist, *Monsieur*, tell us what you know."

He looked at her, seemed to make up his mind, and continued, "Louisiana's present governor, Perier, does not handle the Indians as well as his predecessor, Governor Bienville. Bienville made some mistakes, but he knew when to be firm and when to flatter them and give them presents. Perier is indecisive and does neither. This gives the British a free hand to stir up trouble."

At this point Suzanne had begun to look glassy-eyed. Captain seemed to talk directly to a fascinated Madeleine. "To make matters worse, he is unwise in his appointment. He has just reappointed Etcheparre, an incredibly vicious fool, to Fort Rosalie, right in the middle of the Natchez Indians. He did this even after Fort Rosalie settlers had brought Etcheparre before the council for greed and cruelty. It makes for potential trouble."

Sister Pauline remembered, "But you did say New Orleans was protected by *les soldats*."

Captain Beauchamp reluctantly admitted, "*Oui*, but actually they are inadequate. Both Bienville and Perier have requested more troops but have never been successful in getting enough."

A gloom fell over the little group. Madeleine tried to cheer up the other women. "I understood that the French get along well with the Indians."

Andre snorted again, then pretended to choke when the captain looked at him pointedly. The captain tried to

be more diplomatic. "It is true that the French are generally better liked than the British or Spanish, but Indians
are not so different from us. They can be as changeable as
the French, and no easier to understand. I will tell you a
story of an Indian princess as an example."

Suzanne asked coyly, "Is it a romantic story? I am
bored with talk of the British and Indians."

You might call it romantic," the captain answered.
"The commander of the French fort in our Illinois territory
wanted to impress his Indian friends and at the same time
show his friends in France some real live Indians. So he
persuaded twelve warriors and the chief's beautiful
daughter to accompany him to Paris."

"Ah, I love the story already," gushed Suzanne.

"The Indians were a huge success in court. They were
dressed up like dolls in the latest fashions and made much
of. The princess was married off to a Sergeant Dubois, elevated to captain for the occasion. The princess was first
converted to Christianity and baptized at Notre-Dame. The
Indians had a wonderful time. They danced on the floor of
the Italian opera and hunted deer in the Bois de Boulogne.
Finally, they sailed for home and were cheered at New Orleans and escorted in state back up river. Dubois took over
his new post at the fort, but his Indian wife started to visit
her people more and more. Then, she and her tribe attacked the fort by surprise and slaughtered everybody in
it, including her husband. The princess shed her French
finery and religion and returned to her old life."

The women looked so forlorn that the captain felt a
little guilty. Madeleine asked him, "Do you have anything
good to say about our new home or its people?"

"*Oui, Mademoiselle*, I have painted too negative a

picture. Louisiana—the whole Mississippi Valley—is the most beautiful, the lushest, the greenest land you have ever seen. And New Orleans, like its people, is a little disreputable, which means she is more tolerant than her stiff-necked Puritan British counterparts at Jamestown and Boston."

Sister Mary said, "I hope our order of Ursuline nuns has had some restraining influence on all this tolerance and gaiety."

"*Certainement*, Sister, the Ursulines have done much good in the short time they have been in New Orleans. They are even more important than wives to Louisiana. They have opened a school for young girls. Even Negro and Indian girls are allowed to be educated there. They also have opened an orphanage and taken over the hospital. But I fear that, in the one year they have been in New Orleans, they have not worked miracles on the city's morals."

Sister Mary argued further, "All the settlers are not the lower life you speak of. I know from the other Sisters' letters that there are many fine respectable French families in Louisiana. Surely they have some influence. Perhaps you do not move in their circles, Captain."

Captain Beauchamp smiled, "*Touché*, Sister. You are right. It is simply that the recent recruits by Law have for the moment outnumbered the respectable people. I have no doubt that the scum will be weeded out. I am also sure that you and your *filles a la casquette* will have a gentling influence on the territory. But you must remember, even the respectable Frenchmen did not leave their pursuit of pleasure behind when they left France."

Chapter 6

Madeleine and Suzanne were the only ones left on the berth reserved for seasick passengers. Suzanne was the patient, Madeleine the nurse. The nuns had insisted on keeping the seasick girls separate for the sake of cleanliness and to discourage nausea by association. The sickroom had frequently been so crowded that a second berth was required, and the girls simply had to double up to provide one. Now, however, after three months at sea, the wind had settled and the ship was relatively steady. All the women except Suzanne had recovered long ago.

Madeleine coldly and efficiently administered wet cloths to the retching Suzanne and cleaned up after her. She begrudged the amount of precious water she had to use on her ungrateful patient. Like the nuns, she knew their store of water was running low. The amount that was left was no longer fresh, having been stored in barrels in the holds for these three months. On Sister Pauline's instructions, she had boiled the water to purify it, having to slip unseen into the forecastle to use the only stove on the ship.

Madeleine had been picked as Suzanne's nurse for two reasons. First, she was a good nurse. After she had recovered so quickly from her own bout with *mal de mer*, she soon learned from the nuns, often sick themselves, how to be an excellent nurse. The nuns marveled that a girl from such a noble family could be so hard working, so quiet and unassuming, expecting no words of praise. She also gained the respect and gratitude of the other girls, except for Suzanne, who became sick earlier and stayed sick longer than anyone else.

Suzanne herself was the other reason for Madeleine's playing nurse. The nuns thought Madeleine needed to be taught a lesson regarding Suzanne. The Sisters had taken advantage of the voyage to encourage the girls' devotion to their religion and to teach them any housewifely skills they were lacking. They found fertile ground in Madeleine. To their surprise, she was better trained in domestic skills than they were. Plus, they found her to be pious and willing to read not only the Bible from cover to cover but any other book available. She was now reading Shakespeare's plays, borrowed by Sister Pauline from Captain Beauchamp's small private library.

Her only faults seemed to be her pride and her open dislike for Suzanne, a dislike that was mutual. The girls sniped at each other constantly. The Sisters gave up on improving Suzanne's soul or mind. The girl's temper had gotten progressively worse during the voyage. But Madeleine was a different story. As penance for a particularly sarcastic exchange with Suzanne, Madeleine was instructed by the nuns to care for the blond girl when she became sick once more.

"Try to contain your retching to the basin, *s'il vous plait*," Madeleine gritted. She longed to be on the deck in the fresh air with the other girls.

When Suzanne had stopped heaving, she retorted, "But you clean up so well. One would think you were accustomed to the job."

Madeleine stuck a wet cloth on Suzanne's forehead with enough force to jar her pretty head and replied, "Some of us learn quickly and perform our duties well— without whining."

Suzanne lay back and panted a little, trying to think of a sharper insult, but not one so sharp that she would lose her nurse. Madeleine watched the other girl's ample bosom rise and fall a little enviously. Her own high, firm breasts were small in comparison, unusual for French-women who prided themselves on their rounded figures. It seemed to Madeleine that the wretched girl's breasts had gotten larger even in the interminable months they had been on this cursed ship. All the other girls had lost weight because of the meager rations, but Suzanne's body seemed to fill out more. Madeleine quickly crossed herself and said two Hail Mary's for her uncharitable and vulgar thoughts.

Suzanne had been watching her contemptuously, "You are so pure and holy; I pity your poor husband-to-be when he takes you to bed."

Her remark stung. Madeleine had tried not the think about her marital duties. Being a farm girl, she knew she must have more knowledge of the earthier aspects of marriage than Suzanne and the other girls. She had seen farm animals mate and heard her own father grunting and panting over her passive, long-suffering mother. Her fastidious tastes were repelled by what she had seen thus far of sex. Whenever she thought of it at all, she pulled a hazy curtain over her mind.

Madeleine was determined not to let Suzanne think she had affected her. She deliberately put on her mask of cool arrogance. "I'm sure I will learn this task as well as any other I have learned. After all, if I can clean up after you, I can do anything, however distasteful. What do you know of this subject anyway? What makes you think you will please your husband, providing you get one?"

This time it was Suzanne's turn to fall silent. She closed her eyes, and a brooding look passed over her face. Madeleine noted the change in the other girl's mood and came close to pitying her. She grudgingly admitted to herself that Suzanne could justifiably be depressed about being sick so often. She got sick even before the storms began, and now the water was relatively calm. The ship seemed barely to be moving. Madeleine wiped her own brow, dampened by the hot humid air in the room, and longed to escape this sour air and the even sourer Suzanne.

Just as she was beginning to dislike her patient again intensely, Suzanne let out a sharp cry. Madeleine resignedly went to her side, thinking she was making a dramatic play for attention, but she quickly saw that Suzanne was not pretending; she was in real pain. Her face went white, and her body doubled in agony.

"Suzanne, I will call for Sister Pauline."

"*Non*, please do not! Please stay with me."

"I promise I will be right back. You are *really* sick. I do not know how to help you."

"*Non*, you must not call anyone. You must not. I beg of

you. Please! I will never say another unkind word to you again."

"But surely you prefer a real nurse. I don't know what is wrong with you. I can't help you. You will be alone for only a moment."

Suzanne shouted in her urgency to stop Madeleine. "*Non*, you will ruin me if you do. If you tell anyone, I swear I will jump overboard. My life will be over anyway."

"What do you mean? What is wrong with you?"

The two girls locked eyes, Suzanne's full of despair and defiance, Madeleine's full of dawning comprehension. Of course, it was obvious. Suzanne's breasts had grown larger, and these bouts of nausea had nothing to do with the gentle rocking of a boat on a calm sea. "Suzanne, are you with child?"

"*Oui*," she hissed, "I hope to soon be *without* child. Please, Madeleine, I am bleeding."

"You are being sacrilegious. You cannot mean you want your own child to die." Then she wondered if she would feel different in Suzanne's situation. A girl with a child—a girl whose honor had been tainted—would stand no chance of finding a husband in Louisiana.

Madeleine saw that Suzanne was wavering between hysteria and the practical need to keep her situation quiet. As much as she disliked the girl, she saw the desperation of her plight and knew she could not tell the nuns. They would be bound by their duty to the church and the Company to exclude Suzanne from the *casquette* girls.

She tried to calm her own fears by reassuring Suzanne. "Please, try to relax. I will take care of you myself. I will tell no one."

Suzanne looked at her with the eyes of a stricken

animal. "Do you promise? Swear that you will tell no one, no matter what happens."

Madeleine reluctantly agreed. "I promise. Now you must try to straighten out and raise your knees so I can examine you."

Madeleine was not sure she was equal to this task. She had helped her father deliver calves and remembered snatches of information dropped by neighboring women when her mother gave birth to her brothers and sisters. She washed her hands and went to work. She overcame her distaste and washed the blood off Suzanne. She put a clean linen under her just as her body went into convulsions.

"Oh, the pain, the pain, I cannot stand it! Please stop the pain!"

Madeleine was gritting her teeth so hard she could not reply. She was busy receiving a small bloody, unmoving mass from Suzanne's body. She wrapped the fetus in the sheet, thinking it looked more like a piece of cow's liver than it did a human. She laid it gently beside the bed; then she washed her hands, trying not to think.

Suzanne was nearly unconscious from shock and pain, but some small instinct for survival kept her alert. "Madeleine," she said faintly but urgently, "you must get rid of it. Please, or I might as well die too. Please, I will do anything for you."

"I will take care of it," Madeleine replied grimly. "Now swallow this. It will help you sleep." She gave Suzanne a drop of laudanum from Sister Pauline's small secret supply in the medicine trunk from the closet, a supply only she and the Sisters knew about.

Suzanne, exhausted from her ordeal and knowing she

could trust Madeleine to keep her word, fell asleep quickly. Madeleine resigned herself to the task before her. She knew Suzanne was right about one thing: she would be ruined if anyone else knew about her predicament. Gathering up the bundle beside the bed, she poured a little water over it and mumbled, "I baptize thee in the name of the Father, the Son, and the Holy Spirit." Then she put the bundle in a half-filled pail.

As Madeleine was leaving the cabin, she nearly ran into Sister Pauline in the hatchway. "Why, Madeleine, my dear, I came to relieve you. Please give me that pail. I will empty it for you."

Madeleine's heart nearly stopped. "*Non, merci*, Sister, I will finish the job myself. I will just throw this overboard and be right back. Suzanne is sleeping now, so I think it's best not to disturb her. She has had a rough time. If you don't mind, I would like to stay with her tonight."

"You want to continue nursing her? But, my child, that is not necessary. You have done your penance."

"I know, Sister, but I wish to stay by her side. I have had time to search my soul, and I believe you were right. I have been unkind to her and I would like to make amends. I have discovered she has many unusual qualities, and we have become closer. Please, she now wants no one else to care for her."

Sister Pauline stared at Madeleine. Why, the girl must be giddy from fatigue. It was not like her to chatter like a magpie. Still she had obviously benefited from her punishment so she would indulge her whim. "Very well, as you wish. But you must call me if Suzanne awakens and becomes fretful. I know she can be difficult."

With that Madeleine was in hearty agreement. She

took her leave, climbed the ladder to the deck and, with a practiced twist of her wrist, tossed the contents of the pail overboard. Her only witness was a fascinated captain, watching her from the quarterdeck.

A few days after Suzanne's "sick spell," she was back to normal and in good spirits. She and Madeleine maintained a cool truce. The other girls were curious at the change in them. They were surprised at Madeleine's and Suzanne's new cordiality and missed the excitement of their arguments, for there was little of interest on the voyage. They still kept their distance from the more reserved Madeleine but frequently questioned Suzanne about what had gone on in the sickroom the day Madeleine was her nurse. Suzanne would merely toss her blond curls and flippantly remark, "Oh, she is not as bad as I thought."

Madeleine often caught Suzanne watching her, waiting for her to give her away; but Madeleine never indicated by word or lifted eyebrow that anything had ever been amiss. She never questioned Suzanne about the child or its father. After a week had passed and she realized her secret was safe, Suzanne began to relax. In an effort to mend fences with the other women, she began to charm them with lavish compliments and juicy gossip about Louis XV's court, with which she claimed to be familiar.

One sunny day, some of the girls had dragged empty wooden barrels onto their usual place at the rear of the quarterdeck and were sewing under the watchful eyes of Sister Pauline and Sister Mary. Suzanne managed to maneuver her barrel close to Madeleine's and engaged her in a low conversation. "Madeleine, you have never asked how I came to be in my, uh, unfortunate situation; yet I know you must have wondered."

"It seemed clear to me *how* you came to be with child. The particulars are not my concern. You do not have to worry; I will keep my promise."

Suzanne hurriedly assured her, "I know you will. Whatever our differences have been, I have always known you are an honorable person. That is why I trusted you."

Madeleine did not mention the obvious, that Suzanne had no choice but to trust her. Suzanne continued, "Having such a high opinion of you, I would not want you to have a low one of me. I feel compelled to offer you some explanation."

"But I assure you it is not necessary."

"But it is." Suzanne's blue eyes filled with tears, which she daintily dabbed with a lace handkerchief. "My dear friend, I was taken advantage of."

"You mean you were raped?" Madeleine asked in surprise. She knew no delicate way to put it.

Suzanne looked equally surprised. "Why, yes, that exactly what happened. I was raped. It was an old friend of my father's. He was rich, so my father wanted me to marry him and arranged for us to be together a great deal. He was old and ugly and had spindly legs, but his arms were strong. That is how he overpowered me." She began to warm to her story. "I was in love with this man's handsome younger son who, alas, had no inheritance. Oh, my, but the son seated a horse well. He said I rode so well I seemed a part of the horse."

Madeleine prompted her gently, "And the older gentleman, the one who overcame you?"

"Ah, yes, him. He caught me in the garden, just four months ago, between the rose bushes and the dahlias. I was wearing my favorite pink day dress. Oh, it was terrible." She shuddered delicately. "When I told my father what happened, he didn't believe me and still wanted me to marry his friend, but I hated him for seizing my virtue, so I refused. Then, two months later, I realized I was pregnant."

"How sad," Madeleine said, wondering if it were the old friend or the son who had gotten her pregnant.

Suzanne sighed, "That is why I decided to go to Louisiana Territory. I could not bear to drag my family through a scandal. Still, you can understand why I do not regret losing the child."

"Yes, of course."

"And you understand why you must keep my secret. Or my sacrifice will have been for nothing."

Madeleine did understand. Though she did not see Suzanne's sacrifice, she understood the need for secrets and the need to make a fresh start.

Chapter 7

A few days outside of Louisiana, the crew as well as the women anxiously awaited their first sight of land. There was a fair wind, heavy with the moisture of the tropics, as *les Belles Soeurs* entered the Gulf of Mexico, and the ship was running dead before the wind.

Captain Beauchamp was as anxious as anyone. As he strode across the deck, his rolling gait compensated for the moderate swell as the ship's bow overtook and rode the oncoming waves. The humid breeze sang through the rigging while he kept a critical eye on the activity surrounding him. The watch had just changed and the crew was working out the kinks of inactivity from their cramped sleeping areas. The *les Belles Soeurs*, as with all ships of the time, did not have specific crew quarters; so the men had to sleep in any nook or cranny to be found aboard ship.

"Andre, bring her up into the wind; round forward!" The headsails were braced around and the jibs sheeted to starboard. As she came up on the new tack, the crew braced the yards and the headsails met her.

"Set the spanker!" yelled Andre to a responsive crew that had learned to work as one during the many days' passage. The wind filled the sails as the ship came around, the main sail was set, and the crew got ready to clear up as she settled on a port tact.

"Smartly done, Andre. To see the crew at work, you would think they were on the Admiral's deck with the fear of the lash goading them on."

"*Oui, Capitaine*, the crew is as quick as any fleet complement. Our gun training has been as good as anything His Majesty's peacocks could do. At this rate we could reach New Orleans six days early."

"Andre, you have enough years at sea to know better than predict our arrival. Nature has no interest in our insignificant schedules."

"Sail ho! Captain," interrupted the lookout.

"Where away?" responded the captain.

"Two points off the starboard bow, and she is closing fast."

"Can you make out her colors?"

"No.... Aye! A pirate brig, sir!"

"Andre, beat to quarters; run out the guns! Perhaps when she sees our teeth she'll run.

Load number 3 and 4 guns with chain-shot," ordered Jean Paul, this to play havoc with the pirate ship's rigging and, if lucky, to destroy its ability to maneuver. "Load 1 and 2, 5 and 6 with ball, and run out the port battery as well. Keep shot handy if we close. Bo'sun, issue arms to the men, Gunner, your best marksman on 5 and 6. Hold your fire until ordered. Men, a gold sovereign to dismast the rogue!"

Then he thought of his passengers and groaned, "*Sacre bleu!* Jean, make sure all the women are below and out of sight. Tell them they must not be seen no matter what they hear above." The boy ran below at once to warn the women.

The crew reacted with swift economy to the captain's orders. The women, huddled together in terror in their cabins, could hear the creak and rumble as the heavy cannons were manhandled to their firing position. The men sweated and grunted with exertion. Powder was measured; rammer and sponge were reamed into the muzzle; powder, wads and ball were loaded. The men gave fleeting thought to the certainty that, in minutes, red hot shot would slam their ship, gouging great hunks of wood, setting deadly razor-sharp splinters flying. But, with this crew of experienced hands, it was only a fleeting thought. The task at hand of defending their only link with continuing life, their ship, demanded all their attention.

Duvall, the chief gunner, cursed his gun-layers to be faster. His face was scowling, fearsome-looking to the men. He had an ugly red scar that began at the bridge of his nose, cut to a patch where his left eye once was and continued to his temple. The scar was a small souvenir of a waterfront dispute over a poxy whore. He had survived the bloody fight that cost him only an eye, but the filthy weasel Corsican was not able to say the same. Duvall had traded an eye for the Corsican's life.

He shouted, "Louis, look to the port battery. Make damn sure when the firing begins that those sons of rabid whore-mongers don't load powder before they swab."

"Aye, Duvall, I'll not allow the cannon to blow up in

their sweet faces," replied Louis as he began to cross the deck.

Guns were run out; activity quieted. The gun-layers leaned over the muzzles, sighting the pirates' brig, which on a beam reach was coming fast. The lull before the storm, thought the captain. Little did the pirates know what was in store for them. *Les Belles Soeurs* appeared to be an innocent merchant, an easy prey. But it was captained by one of the most experienced fighters on the seas and crewed by the most dangerous scum, murderers and naval-trained gun handlers France could offer. It was an adversary even Lord St. Vincent, the great British naval hero, would mark.

The powder-boys eyed the captain nervously. Mere children, they had never experienced anything more fearsome than the bo'sun's anger. Captain Beauchamp represented the father few of them had ever known. He was stern with them but the love they had for him was inspired by his gentle strength. They knew that whatever came—storms, pirates, or the Devil from hell himself—Beauchamp would win the day and do it with style.

Jean Paul returned the gaze of the powder-boy on number 6 gun. He thought, "Do not be concerned, my friend; a trifling pirate is no match for us this day." He knew he had selected his crew well. The owners allowed him total latitude. He had Duvall from the *Challenger*; Louis, a one-time murderer who had run to the sea to escape the justice awaiting satisfaction for his crimes; and Andre, who had sailed every sea on the charts. The rest of the crew was the best money could buy. Dupre and his partner were unusual owners. To them the extra expense of a top crew made good financial sense. One lost cargo because of inept hands would wipe out a number of voyages' profits.

Jean Paul looked past the powder-boy to the ship. Andre had prepared her well; the brig was still well out of range. The two ships were on a converging course. If he maintained his course, the pirate would have to tact to bring a broadside to bear. The pirate vessel was faster but carried fewer guns. The other captain must either hit and run, or go for a stern shot where *les Belles Soeurs* was most vulnerable. If he waited until the last moment, he could bring his ship about and deliver his broadside on the first pass.

"Andre, prepare to bring her about when we are within a chain's length. We'll give them a broadside they'll be long forgetting. The fools think we are for the taking."

The pirate fired his bow-chaser, perhaps expecting a quick surrender. It dropped short of the mid-ship. The unsuspecting pirate could by now see the guns run out on his prey. Already he must be concerned, for many merchants went unarmed or with fewer guns.

"Duvall, a ranging shot, please," requested Jean Paul in a quiet, confident voice. Number 2 gun roared its pleasure of released gases and iron. It recoiled back to the waiting hands of the gun layers who were preparing a new load before its round had completed its flight. A cheer went up from the other gun layers. The ranging shot had found its mark; it struck the brig just in front of the foremast. At that distance, Jean Paul could see the impact shatter the deck. It wasn't a very damaging blow, but he knew the value of drawing first blood.

"Hold your fire," he commanded, sensing the crew's impatience to fire again. The pirate ship still came bow-up at *les Belle Soeurs'* mid-ship. He must be planning to cut across the stern and fire his cannon into that weaker part of the ship.

Jean Paul ordered his helmsman to fall off a little, making all sails draw, and increased the speed. "On my order, prepare to bring her about."

The pirate ship was closing in, attempting to cut behind him. "Helm's *alee*," he commanded. The helmsman put the wheel down and crewman released the headsheets, while other crewmen hauled the spanker aweather.

"Fire 5 and 6 as they bear," ordered Jean Paul. The two guns released their fury in rapid order, spewing the guts of chemical reaction out their muzzles, the murderous iron death directed at the interloper. The smoke from the two spent cannons shrouded the deck. Captain Beauchamp stepped forward to be ready to order his port guns to action once the tact was rounded. A shattering crash behind him caught his attention. Screams of agony rose from the helmsman as he clung desperately to the wheel. A shot from the pirate had grooved the deck and smashed into the bulwark creating a deadly shower of splinters and wood fragments.

Jean Paul rushed over to the wheel taking control. The helmsman fell to the deck with a gaping hole in his stomach. He screamed in terror as he saw his own intestine. Blood ran onto the deck from the wound. A number of jagged edged splinters were imbedded in his face, one squarely centered where the man's eye had been. Then the screaming stopped.

"Bos'un, take the helm. Haul the mainsail, you lubbers." The ship's forward movement slowed as her bow was forced over to port. This was the vulnerable part of the maneuver, and the pirate captain took quick advantage of his swifter keel. He, seeing he would be unable to cross Jean Paul's stern, had begun to tact on the shot that killed the helmsman. Now he began firing into the mid-ships of the turning merchantman.

Jean Paul ordered his men to fire when the pirate filled the gun layer's sight. None could yet bear. The captain of the pirate brig ordered his guns, and two iron balls slammed *les Belle Soeurs* amidships, the first striking just above the gun port of the number 5 gun. The two-ton gun lifted from the deck and smashed into the gun crew, squashing the head of the powder boy with a hollow *clop*. Two of the gunners lay pinned beneath the cannon. One stared uncomprehendingly at where his legs were crushed by the barrel of the cannon. The numbing shock he experienced mercifully short-circuited his nerves from informing his brain of the trauma. The other screamed out his rage and agony, for just moments before he had stood by, his weapon drawing false confidence from its latent power, knowing absolutely that nothing could harm him or his massive, indestructible charge.

Below deck the women huddled together praying and crying. Occasionally one would scream in terror. Madeleine, stiff with fright, prayed silently, her nimble fingers working quickly over the rosaries. She told herself that even living in her parents' hut would be better than dying at the hand of pirates. She and the other girls had whispered in mock fear at night about being captured by pirates. Now their fear was real.

The pirates' second round smashed into the foremast foot, creating havoc with the deck crew. One sailor was knocked from this tenuous perch in the rigging by the shock of the white-hot ball striking the mast. His body slammed the deck with enough force to break every one of his major bones. Other members of the crew lifted bleeding bundles, which moments before had been their mates, from the deck to take them below. The Sisters and Madeleine were grateful finally to have something to do but wait. They quickly lay aside the dead and worked tirelessly to save the barely living. Madeleine, just like the other girls was as horrified at the bloody, grisly condition of their patients, but she gritted her teeth and used every ounce of energy and intelligence she possessed to ease their pain and heal their wounds.

Blood and torn pieces of flesh covered the deck near the foremast. Duvall, a lopsided grin showing his pleasure at the action and mayhem, ordered the stunned deck crew nearest him to man the sheets released by the dead crew. "Now, we don't want a little noise and blood to spoil our gunners' aim at that nasty little brigand, do we?" he asked of a crewman bleeding from a head wound. "You have but a small crease in your head, my friend, lots of blood but not much damage, so grab hold of this and heave."

Les Belles Soeurs completed her tact and was straightening out, the wind an aid in trimming her. Now our damage will be done, thought Jean Paul. "Fire the port battery," he yelled. Before the order cleared his vocal cords, the remaining guns exploded their wrath. The iron shot slammed and stowed the pirate ship. The chain shot tore rigging apart. Crosstrees and yards fell on the pirate crew, breaking bones and tearing flesh. One of the pirates' guns blew up, spewing iron shrapnel into the surrounding men, killing and maiming them in the flicker of a fuse spark.

Sails fell and covered the men who fought in panic to get clear of the heavy canvas.

Andre had trained his men well; they could re-load their bronze beasts in less than a minute. *Les Belles Soeurs* let fly another broadside. One shot struck her lower foremast, splitting it neatly, bringing down rigging, blocks, men, canvas, and assorted death to the crewman below it. The pirate ship burned; the white-hot shot had ignited canvas and wood alike. Jean Paul watched with professional interest as the opposing captain tried desperately to save his ship. The pirates' remaining crew, some bleeding from deadly wounds, were cutting away fallen rigging. Others fought the blazes consuming the ship. The pirate captain, giving no quarter in his long and deadly career, expected none from Jean Paul.

Jean Paul could clearly see his adversary. The pirate captain was almost as tall as he. Blond hair pushed out from under his hat. His beard was almost white from the sun's bleaching it over thousands of miles and days at sea. Jean Paul felt no compassion for the pirate. Had the pirate had the opportunity he would have cut Beauchamp's living heart from his chest while boiling his crew in seawater. And the *casquette* girls would have prayed for death if the crew of the burning ship had them for only an hour. He tried not to think of the fine, long-limbed Madeleine in their hands.

"Andre, another broadside into the cur—let us be done with this."

The death blow erupted from *les Belle Soeurs*, smashing full strength into the brig. The instant of impact shattered the brig's back and, as the ship started to sink, convulsed into a deafening roar as the gunpowder stores blew. A brief boil in the sea and nothing remained but bits of wood, nothing discernable as being from a ship.

No cheers went up from the crew. An unnatural quiet fell over the ship. Then the moans of the wounded were heard. Orders began to fly from all points on the deck. The engagement over; it was time to put the ship in order.

"Andre, have the cook bring some food and whiskey from the galley," cried Jean Paul in relief. "And go tell the girls that they and the future of Louisiana are safe."

Chapter 8

Madeleine stood on the quarterdeck of the ship just as the sun was setting. She was wearing a light-yellow cotton dress to withstand the humid August heat. She, like the other passengers and the crew, had settled into a calm anticipation of the end of their voyage. They had weathered storms, seasickness, scanty food rations, both hot and cold weather, and pirates and felt lucky to have survived. Although there was still a careful distance between crew and passengers, of necessity under the watchful eyes of the nuns and the captain, there was now a mutual respect between the two groups. Madeleine especially was singled out for admiration because of her cool manner under the pirates' attack. Several wounded crew members owed their lives to her tireless nursing.

As Madeleine watched the sunset, she was both longing for and dreading the sight of land. She had mixed feelings about the voyage ending. As uncomfortable as the ship was, she knew she had made an important niche for herself here. She had found companionship and acceptance that she had never had before. Would she find this in Louisiana, she wondered? Though she knew she was better able to cope with a primitive life than the other girls, she wondered if even she could survive a frontier as fraught with danger as the captain and his crew described. Like the other girls, she had never seen an Indian or an alligator before. She had no skills for combatting them and felt at a disadvantage.

She also hated to admit to herself that she would miss Captain Beauchamp. She knew no more about the mysterious captain than she did before. She had carefully avoided being alone with him again; but, whenever she saw him striding along the deck giving orders, she felt an undercurrent running between them. Surely he felt it too. Is he married? Is that why he had not tried to court her?

She shook her head as if to rid it of burdensome thoughts. Even if he had pursued her, which he had not, she did not want to live on board a ship. Nor did she want to spend her life waiting on shore most of the year for her husband to come home. Not that he had indicated in any way that the thought of marriage had even occurred to him. Suddenly she jumped at hearing the captain's voice, thinking for a moment he had spoken aloud in her thoughts; but she realized he was below talking with Andre.

"*Mon Dieu*, Andre, I will be glad to be rid of this cargo. I don't know how much longer I can keep my woman-hungry crew away from those *filles a la casquette*. The French government will have our heads on a platter if we do not deliver them intact to their future husbands."

"*Oui, Capitaine*, the governor has pinned all his hopes on these *casquette* girls to settle down the soldiers and colonists," Andre stated, "but men of New Orleans seem to prefer chasing after Indian squaws and prostitutes."

"Well, few people believed his stories of paradise where one could pick up gold and silver off the ground. Both John Law and his predecessor, Anthony Crozat, had to resort to extreme measures to get colonists. Before John Law left the Company, we brought over some of the worse scum I have ever seen, even in the lowest dives of Paris."

Andre nodded, a little bored with this conversation, then began to smile at his own thoughts. "*Capitaine*, remember that red-headed hellion, Marie. What a woman she was! She alone must have kept the whole crew happy—and built up quite a nest egg to start her new life."

The captain smiled too. "She is trying to go respectable now. The last time we were in New Orleans she was the nightly companion of an aristocratic young soldier. We must take care not to talk about her activities aboard our ship. Let her have her chance."

"Well, she was a hell of a lot more exciting than the German passengers."

"Actually the only passengers I really enjoyed were the Germans because they were no trouble. They kept the ship clean and never complained about anything."

Andre agreed, "*Oui*, they were a sturdy lot. And such hard workers. If it were not for them being there now, we would have a lot of trouble getting a supply of fresh vegetables and fruit when we come into port."

"*Vraiment*, Andre, I'm afraid our countrymen are more interested in gambling and drinking than in farming. They were not prepared for survival in Louisiana."

"The governor has pinned a lot of hopes on these *filles a la casquette* to settle down the soldiers and colonists," Andre stated doubtfully.

"*Oui*," Captain Beauchamp chuckled, "I hope Bienville knows he got his wish for decent women to keep the men from chasing after indecent ones."

"I think that dark-haired, long-legged de Mandeville girl could keep you out of the woods. I have seen you looking at her like you wished those long legs were wrapped around your neck."

The captain gave his first mate a look that should have silenced him, but Andre was not looking his way and continued, "Ah, *Capitaine*, you can have that stiff-necked snob. I will take that blond Suzanne any day or night. She has a damn sight more flesh to dip into."

"She is a typical Frenchwoman who will quickly turn to fat. She obviously likes her cuisine. Even worse, she is the kind who expects an easy life. Now Mademoiselle de Mandeville, underneath that genteel manner, is lean and tough. She will have to be to survive the life she will have in Louisiana."

"That may be, *Capitaine*, but I would still pick the one with the big breasts."

Madeleine's cheeks burned at their remarks. She rushed down the stairs on the opposite side of the main deck to get away from their voices, only to run straight into the captain climbing up the stairs to investigate the sound of her footsteps. As he had done once before, he caught her arms to keep her from falling. This time, however, they fought the pull toward each other and remained distant and formal.

"*Bonjour, Mademoiselle*, you seem in a hurry."

"Let me pass, *s'il vous plait*," Madeleine said coldly.

"Ah, you heard us talking, *n'est-ce pas?*"

"Heard who talking, *Monsieur?*"

"Don't try to fool me. We have offended you with our crude talk. For a peasant girl, you certainly have fine aristocratic sensibilities."

"One does not need to be of the nobility to wish to be treated respectfully," Madeleine replied.

"That is very important to you—respect—is it not?"

"No more than to anyone else."

"But especially to you, my proud girl. I think that is what gets you up in the morning and keeps you going," he said.

"Do your duties as captain include reading my mind, *Monsieur?* And what gets you up in the morning?"

The captain pulled Madeleine back up the stairs and finally answered her, still holding her arm, but gently now. "It is being a captain that gets me out of bed. Nothing else ever has. No woman has ever distracted me from the sea for very long. Sailing is what I live for."

Madeleine turned her face away from him looking intently at the setting sun, now an orange blob on the horizon.

"Did you never try to live on land?" She asked softly.

"*Oui*, but never successfully. I was a fish out of water. Sooner or later I made a stench. I never stay more than a few weeks on land. Even then I get restless."

Madeleine looked back at him and asked directly, "Why are you telling me this, *Monsieur?*"

"Because we will soon be sighting land. You will marry and start a new life."

"I still do not understand the connection."

"Don't pretend with me, Madeleine. Play a role with the others but not with me. I want you to know why I cannot marry again."

"Again?" Madeleine's face registered shock and hurt for a minute before she closed off her expression from him.

"*Oui*, my wife is dead." This time it was the captain's turn to look at the sunset, now barely visible as a dark orange glow.

"Dead?" Madeleine guiltily felt relief mixed with pity for Captain Beauchamp.

"Yes, and, Madeleine, it is because of me that she and our unborn child are both dead. I should never have married. I never will again."

"But surely their deaths are not your fault." Madeleine wanted to take his face in her hands and comfort him.

"You must trust me when I say it *was* my fault. Madeleine, I was away so much of the time, home only a couple of times a year and just for a few weeks then. My wife was very young and not very strong. When she became with child, I think the loneliness and responsibility were too much for her. One day after she had waved goodbye to me from the dock, she waited until the ship was out of sight, until she was alone, and just walked out into the sea."

Madeleine was shocked. "*Mon Dieu*, how did you know what happened to her then, if she was alone?"

"Someone saw her from a distance through the window of a restaurant. I did not learn of her death until three months later when I returned."

They were both silent for a moment. Madeleine ached to comfort him but did not know how. Finally, he said in a tight, impersonal voice, "So you see why I would never put another woman in that position again. Very few captains marry, and those who do invariably regret it."

"Perhaps you are right, *Monsieur*," Madeleine too became withdrawn. In spite of his being visibly upset, she wondered if this was his way of avoiding entanglements with female passengers foolish enough to fall in love with him. Not that it had gone that far with her, she thought with determined gratitude.

"Is this your way of saying *au revoir*?" she asked.

Captain Beauchamp saw the hurt behind her masked face and gathered her resistant body in his arms. "I could not say goodbye to you without letting you know that I see your worth. You are an extraordinary woman. I know you will endure quite well in this swamp you are going to. I envy the man who marries you."

Madeleine put up a token struggle and then relaxed and luxuriated in the feel of his arms around her. "Again, *pourquoi*, why do you say this to me now?"

"Because you have tempted me more than any other woman to change my mind about marrying and leaving the sea." He stroked her neck lightly.

"But you have obviously resisted the temptation," she said, her neck prickling from his touch.

"Not easily, *ma cherie*, not easily and not lightly." He pulled her head to his shoulder and kissed her hair lightly. "My thoughts go with you. If you ever need me for anything, I come to New Orleans a couple of times a year. You need but to send a message."

Madeleine could not resist lifting her head as he bent his to her. Before their lips could touch, they heard an excited voice calling, "Land ho! Land ho!"

Chapter 9

Madeleine shared the lead barge going up the Mississippi River with Sister Pauline, Suzanne, Simone, and Delphine. Looking back, she could see the ten other barges and pirogues transporting the other nuns and *casquette* girls from the harbor of La Balize, where *les Belles Soeurs* had landed, to their destination *La Nouvelle Orleans*. Madeleine was glad she was not in one of the pirogues, which were no more than canoes made of large hollowed-out logs.

She and the other women felt refreshed from their rest at La Balize. They finally had enough water to take a whole bath and wash their clothes. Even though the water was brackish and foul smelling, it seemed reasonably sanitary. They were able to wash out the stale stench that came from months aboard ship. What a luxury to feel almost clean again! Of course, in the near tropical heat, they would not feel clean for long.

Like the other girls, Madeleine at first had thought they would sail in the ship directly from the Gulf of Mexico up the Mississippi to New Orleans. But she remembered that Captain Beauchamp had explained to them the difficulty of large ships getting to New Orleans because of their running aground on the Mississippi's ever-shifting sand bars. He said that, while a few large ships did indeed go upriver, he was too concerned about their safety to risk it and preferred to transfer them to smaller boats. So the passengers of *les Belles Soeurs* had to wait at La Balize two days until the lighter vessels arrived to fetch them.

This five-day trip up the Mississippi had certainly initiated them to their new homeland, Madeleine thought. They had stopped each night and camped on the bank, trying to sleep, but few of the girls had ever slept outdoors before. None had ever been plagued by the hordes of pesky mosquitoes that attacked their tender flesh. They had to sleep under a netting, or *baire*, to get any peace from them. Their boatmen had constructed this protective *baire* by bending long canes and fixing both ends over their mattresses. Then they covered the frame with linens tucked in all around. Even so, a few persistent insects got through.

Another threat, much more frightening, was the huge, strange-looking, lizard-like animals that the oarsmen called *alligators*. The women had seen these creatures swimming beside the barges and sunning themselves on the riverbanks. Their jaws looked incredibly wide and strong, and they had lithe, supple bodies, some of which were over twelve feet long. They could easily swallow a man—or woman—in one gulp, Madeleine feared.

In spite of the problems, Madeleine was glad to be on land again, *any* land. Only the guides' warnings about poisonous snakes they called *moccasins* and wild animals kept her from venturing into the forest. When she walked alone at twilight along the riverbank, the other women sat huddled in misery at the campsite. As the dusk light faded the riverbank into shadows, Madeleine met some more of the inhabitants of the primitive but beautiful land. Struggling through dense bushes, she looked down and mistook a twisted, gnarled root for one of the *moccasin* snakes and, in her fright and recoil, tripped over another root and fell onto the damp earth.

There, not one foot from her nose, was the largest rat she had ever seen in her life. With her heart pounding out the cadence of her terror, she locked eyes with the equally frightened creature. It recoiled from her, rising on its haunches slightly and baring its teeth; but it made no attempt to attack. Realizing that, if it were going to attack it would already have done so, Madeleine began to relax somewhat while she regained her breath and noted that the rat was different somehow from any she had ever seen. Mostly white with brown patches, it looked a great deal like a rat in general form; yet its size, some eighteen inches in body length, plus its long snout, told her that it could not be just a rat. After a short interval of eyeing one another suspiciously, the critter turned and slowly disappeared into the underbrush. Later, while telling the story to the guide, who laughed uproariously, Madeleine discovered that the creature was indeed not a rat, but rather an *opossum*, a nocturnal animal that came out to feed at sundown. The incident made Madeleine wonder what other surprises were in store for her.

On the last day of their barge trip, Madeleine strained to see the riverbanks as they drew nearer to New Orleans.

She had no interest in the river itself, only in the land. She wondered how Captain Beauchamp could bear to be away from solid land most of his life. She thought back to her last sight of the vessel with Captain Beauchamp standing on the quarterdeck of his ship watching them float away. She wondered if she would ever see him again and could not help but feel a tremendous loss. She tried to concentrate on what Sister Pauline was saying to her instead of remembering her last conversation with the captain aboard *les Belles Soeurs*.

"What a great brown flood of a river this Mississippi is!" Sister Pauline exclaimed.

"*Vraiment*, remember how shocked we were to see these muddy waters mingle with the blue waters of the Gulf," Madeleine replied.

All the women were a little subdued, wondering what lay ahead for them. They were happy to be off the turbulent waters of the Atlantic. To Madeleine, the murky Mississippi seemed somehow more manageable than the Atlantic Ocean, yet at the same time powerful and mysterious, hiding its secrets from her. She watched again with interest as they passed by the banks, about a mile apart. How green and lush the land was here! Dense foliage lined the riverbanks. Madeleine got the impression that all of the Mississippi Valley was a forest. After camping at night on the edge of that forest, most of the women were convinced that Louisiana was a jungle.

She was relieved to see occasional farms and plantations scattered infrequently along the river's edge. Some plantations had moss-covered live-oak trees all the way from the main house to the river. She fantasized about living on a plantation. How different that would be from her life so far, she thought. She wondered if she might marry a man who lived in one of these houses—wood in structure, usually unpainted, a story and a half high, and nearly always raised on a high platform, apparently as protection against periodic flooding from the river—not exactly the de Mandeville estate but certainly better than her parents' hovel.

Frequently, people belonging to the houses, mostly Negroes and children, barefoot and scantily dressed for summer, ran from the houses or fields to the edge of the river and waved at them. The women waved back enthusiastically, feeling a little better at being welcomed.

"Look, Madeleine," cried Sister Pauline, "we must be coming upon the English Turn. That means we are almost to New Orleans."

Sure enough they were beginning to round a large hairpin curve they were told was a famous landmark just south of New Orleans. Just before they straightened out of the curve, they could easily see the last pirogue of *casquette* girls excitedly waving at them.

"I wonder why it is called English Turn," commented Suzanne.

"It is a strange name for a French possession," agreed Madeleine. "Captain Beauchamp told me an interesting story about the name."

"Captain seemed to tell you a lot of stories," Suzanne said in a honeyed tone. Delphine and Simone tittered, a little hysterical at the excitement of finally seeing New Orleans.

"*Mes enfants!*" Sister Pauline gently admonished.

Madeleine continued with her story as if she had never been interrupted. "It was named after a British expedition sent to explore the Mississippi. The British were interested, of course, because of our first French settlement here."

Suzanne questioned impatiently, "Why *of course*? Why would the British be interested in *our* settlement?"

Madeleine explained, "They were interested because they want control of North America. One of the British ships was becalmed at this bend in the river. Ironically Governor Bienville came upon them by accident. When he found out that the British were not even sure they were on the Mississippi, he told them the river was much farther west. So they left, never to return—or at least *these* British never returned—but the name stuck."

Suzanne sidled closer to Madeleine and whispered, "Speaking of Captain Beauchamp, did all those long walks on the deck produce nothing from him but stories about the Mississippi? *Ma cherie*, I don't know what I would do if I were rejected by a man after I had so obviously shown a preference for him."

"The way you throw yourself at men, I should think you were accustomed to rejection," retorted Madeleine.

Sister Pauline, suspecting trouble brewing between the two girls, chirped, "Ah, *mes jeunes filles*, look at those lovely trees on the banks. See how their branches bend over and touch the water." She wondered what happened to their short-lived friendship.

"Them trees is willers, ma'am," volunteered Hank Davis, their Kentuckian bargeman, called a *Kaintuck* by the other men. Hank could understand a little French but could not speak it, so Sister Pauline had to translate for him.

"*Willers*, Monsieur?"

"No'm, *will-ohs*," he said suspiciously, thinking she was mocking him.

"Ah, *mais oui*, willows. *Bien sur*."

"Comin' up on New Orleans," shouted the Kentuckian.

Just ahead was the Crescent City, sometimes called that because the constant movement of the river had shaped its banks into the form of the moon in its first quarter. The women strained their eyes to get a glimpse at last of the famous *La Nouvelle Orleans*.

Part II.
New Orleans, August 1728

Chapter 10

In the 1720s, New Orleans was like a sleazy young slut enthusiastically peddling her limited wares. She was rough and bawdy and ready for anything—anything except restraint. And her inhabitants, most of them, seemed interested mainly in drinking and brawling and sampling her wares, while looking for some way, no matter how devious, to make some easy money, often by cheating or murdering other clients.

Madeleine, the nuns, and the other *casquette* girls crowded forward as they arrived at the *quai,* or dockside, to get their first look at New Orleans. It was hardly the "little Versailles" that government's agents had described at home, and the women swallowed hard to mask their disappointment at its size. A huge levee almost obscured the buildings in the city near the docks. Off to the left, they could see two large warehouses angling away from the levee; to the right of the town proper were several log buildings nestled together—the quarters for the small army detachment in New Orleans. Between these two was the *city*—about 130 ramshackle wooden structures, which, mostly single-story, seemed to have been thrown together by whim and located with little sense of symmetry in relation to others. Madeleine noted with a sigh of distaste that they looked terribly flimsy, as if a good strong wind could blow them away. At least, she thought, looking with a farm girl's eye, the lots for the houses are large enough to allow room for generous gardens.

To the women's surprise, they were met by both enthusiastic cheering and equally loud jeering. The soldiers and settlers, including the few wives, were delighted to finally see some decent marriageable women. The crowd also contained some less decent women, taken from prisons and city streets in France. They were jealous and resentful of the attention being paid to the new arrivals. It seemed to Madeleine that all of the thousand or so New Orleans colonists were at the *quai* to greet them.

Chafing from the heat even in her light-blue cotton dress, she shrank back a little from the boisterous attention. Suzanne, however, was in her element. She preened before the crowd, catching many masculine eyes on her red brocade dress. Madeleine wondered nervously if she would be able to carry off her masquerade as a lady. As she stepped from the barge, she forced herself to hold her head high and look steadily at the crowd and the town behind them. Though partly in a daze, she was aware that the town was much smaller than they had been led to believe. It wasn't much bigger than the country village near her parents. She almost gasped aloud in disappointment.

Mon Dieu, she thought, there can't be many more than

a hundred buildings here, and the streets are unpaved. How does one get about in all that mud? I'm glad I didn't believe the streets were paved with gold as some of the girls did.

She had little time to think about her disappointment, for just then she heard the shrill shriek of the girls in front of her and jumped involuntarily. Following their frightened gazes, she saw one of those *gators*, as the bargemen had called them, amble lazily across the street some thirty yards away. Some of the men, as if to show their bravery and worth to the women, began throwing clods of mud at the reptile, who turned, yawned his gaping mouth at the assemblage, and waddled calmly back into the river. Madeleine looked at the crowd of locals and saw that they seemed to be enjoying the incident.

Her level gaze was met by hundreds of hungry male eyes. She had never seen such a strange mixture of people in one place—elaborately dressed men and women, barefoot slaves in rags, hard-faced ruffians, and gaudily dressed, boldly made-up women. Madeleine was relieved to see that the crowd also contained some plainly dressed men, who must be sober faced farmers, merchants, and craftsmen. She saw another type resembling the Kentuckians who brought them upriver: hard-eyed, muscular men in buckskins with knives in their belts. She was alarmed to see that all the people had one thing in common: their clothes, silk or torn buckskin, were splattered with the mud they were standing in, mud as far as she could see.

Madeleine drew nearer to Sister Pauline as some of the bolder men pushed forward to try to talk to her. One held out his hand as if to touch her skirt. She and Sister Pauline matched chilly looks, causing the men to keep their distance. Suzanne, walking behind them and flanked by two nuns anticipating trouble, affected a demure manner now that she saw how easy it was to get attention. She looked shyly from under her eyelashes and took deep breaths as if in fear, causing her full white breasts to strain over the low neckline of her dress.

It was obvious that Madeleine and Suzanne were causing a sensation, for they were by far the prettiest of the girls. Madeleine heard one man whisper to another, "*Quelle bon marche!* What a bargain: looks and virtue in one woman! I wonder why she couldn't find a husband in France."

Madeleine turned furiously toward the voice and saw a handsome young man in an impeccably clean French lieutenant's uniform staring at her. How he managed to stay clean in all that muck was nothing short of miraculous. He was tall, thin, and aristocratic looking, with curly dark hair, brown eyes and sharp, regular features. He lifted his hat to her and inclined his head, never breaking his flattering gaze. Just behind him was a highly rouged, seductively dressed red haired woman, obviously not a lady, looking from him to Madeleine with a less flattering gaze. Madeleine was surprised at the naked rage in the woman's eyes.

The red-haired woman yelled at her, "Why don't you go back to Paris and find a man? Couldn't you handle the competition? Leave mine alone." Then she spat angrily and accurately enough for a stream of spittle to land on Madeleine's clean blue skirt.

Madeleine held her back a little stiffer and kept walking, her insides churning with mortification. She completely ignored the whole incident, refusing even to wipe her dress. This earned her several cheers from the watching crowd. One woman said approvingly, "That girl has *esprit*."

Suzanne said softly from behind, "I am so sorry, Madeleine. I wonder why such a common woman would single you out for attention. Perhaps she is the mistress of the French lieutenant?"

Madeleine was saved from answering by the timely arrival of a welcoming group of Ursuline nuns, recently settled in New Orleans, accompanied by Governor Etienne Perier, the official representative of the Company and the final arbiter of the colony. Madeleine was so preoccupied by the unpleasant scene with the red-haired woman that she barely heard his formal welcoming speech. He and an escort of soldiers accompanied the women the few blocks to the Bienville Hotel at the corner of Bienville and Chartres Streets. One of the few two-story buildings in the city, it was rented for the nuns until their convent was built.

Madeleine was relieved to see that some of the narrow streets were paved by an odd-looking mixture of what the governor said was crushed oyster shells, clay, and sand. He also told them that the mud in the streets was much worse before he had the levee built. He took pride in the fact that the town was now protected not only from excessive mud but from being entirely washed away, as it had been a couple of times by the floods that occurred cyclically every five to seven years. He pointed out the square of streets surrounding the city, bordered by Canal and Esplanade, Old Levee and Rampart Streets, with sixty smaller squares of streets within the larger. "This square," he said, "was designed by the engineer, *le Blond de la Tour*."

The women did not know that the boards they were

walking on had been newly laid on part of their route to keep them from walking in the mud. They were aware, however, that they were wanted and needed in this unruly, primitive town. They had to content themselves with that. There was no turning back.

Chapter 11

By a week after their arrival in New Orleans, even the plainest *casquette* girl had received several proposals. In a town full of bachelors, the sixty respectable girls simply were not enough to go around. Most had accepted and were being married in a mass wedding next Sunday.

Madeleine and Suzanne could afford to take their time in choosing, for they were besieged constantly by proposals. Each afternoon the nuns allowed the girls to receive visitors for a few hours, strictly chaperoned, of course. Madeleine and Suzanne usually had a crowd of eager men around them, vying to fetch them *café au lait* or hot chocolate. When they saw that Madeleine offered them little encouragement and did not flirt, they often deserted her for Suzanne or for one of the other girls with whom they might have more success. Only the more serious and discerning continued to pursue Madeleine. She had yet to meet a suitor who interested her as much as Captain

Beauchamp.

She and Suzanne could not step out of the convent without being gawked at and enthusiastically courted. They each got an offer from Hank Davis, the Kentuckian who had brought them upriver on the barge, not to mention from several other rough frontiersmen who were afraid to brave the formidable Ursuline nuns at visiting hours.

Suzanne obviously enjoyed the attention. She flirted and played one young rake off against the other. She openly admitted to the other girls that she was waiting for the best offer—that is, the offer from the richest man. The good Sisters tried to persuade her that she was doing little more than selling herself, but Suzanne could not be swayed. Even in the short time she had been in New Orleans, she saw how poor women lived, with no servants or slaves to help do their backbreaking work. That was not the life for her.

For once Madeleine was in partial agreement with Suzanne, though she had learned this lesson about women much earlier in her life. Madeleine regretted that she could not afford to marry for love or even for money. She felt she had to marry into an established family in the event her peasant origins were found out. She knew she could not bear to return to a servant's position, not after she had gotten a taste of being treated with respect.

Early each morning before the midday heat set in, Madeleine took a walk along the levee, accompanied by Bette, one of the Negro servants working at the convent. This morning she took a chance on walking along the front part of the city, past the parish church of St. Louis and by the guardhouse and prison. In front of these structures was the *Place d'Armes*, a large clearing sometimes used as a parade ground for the troops or as a meeting place for the townspeople. The rest of the block was used as a marketplace. Madeleine particularly liked the walk along the levee because it was shaded by trees. She soon found that she was not able to walk far before she was confronted by the swamp prairies and tropical, jungle-like forests that met the edge of the city.

She discovered that she had to vary her route each morning or she would have a following of admiring men. She was thinking about proposals from two likely prospects: one from Bernard Hubert, a wealthy but old aide to Governor Etienne Perier, and another from Jean Claude Chauvin, an even wealthier middle-aged merchant, who had caught Suzanne's eye. Both men were considered good catches. Although Madeleine had resigned herself to a loveless marriage, she could not bring herself to even like these two men. She looked out at the Mississippi and thought of Captain Beauchamp. She never thought of him without a pang of regret, but she was too realistic to dream of the impossible.

Her reverie was interrupted by Bette gasping for breath behind her. "*Mademoiselle*, slow down, these old legs can't keep up with you."

Madeleine realized she had been striding along rapidly with her head down, intent in her thoughts. "*Pardonez-moi*, Bette," she apologized and slowed her steps. She looked around her and realized she was growing accustomed to the look and smell of New Orleans. Today the air was already so warm and humid it seemed to form steam on the levee. A two-day rain had added to the humidity. Her yellow cotton dress was damp with perspiration. Fine tendrils of black hair had escaped her bun and clung to her face and neck.

She was particularly thankful for the levee, which prevented the Mississippi from flooding and swamping the whole town in mud and slush. There was already too much mud. She knew that the levee, 5400 feet long and eighteen feet wide, must have taken a lot of time and effort to build. She knew there were few domestic animals like cows or horses in the town—so few, in fact, that there was a strict penalty for killing them.

Just as she approached Chartres Street, she saw what appeared to be a half-naked savage, with dark mahogany skin, coarse black hair, and only two small strips of leather to save him from total nudity. He had decorated himself with a painted bone through his nose, glass beads woven into his hair, and a vermilion stripe down his hairless chest. He stood with his arms folded menacingly in front of her. Madeleine was frozen to the spot. She heard Bette let out a squeal and saw her running back toward the convent faster than she would ever have believed possible.

This must be an Indian, Madeleine thought. She wondered if he were a Natchez come to this spot for revenge. She had heard of little else since her arrival except the expected attack by that tribe. She stood her ground and, for lack of anything better to do, graced the Indian with a deep curtsy.

The Indian's eyes widened slightly in surprise and he barked out a loud guffaw. As he had seen the French do, he gave her a reasonable facsimile of a bow, this time surprising *her*. Then Madeleine heard another masculine laugh behind her, a more musical, less guttural laugh. She turned to see the handsome lieutenant she had seen her first day in New Orleans, the one she had overheard talking about her.

"Lying Boy," he said to the Indian, "you are standing in the lady's way. Let her pass."

As Madeleine walked cautiously past the Indian, the lieutenant gave her the correct version of a gentleman's perfect bow. "*Mademoiselle,* let me introduce myself. I am Lieutenant Jacques Bouligny. Since my servant has frightened away your chaperone, allow me to accompany you back to the convent, *s'il vous plait.*"

Madeleine hesitated and said nothing. She remembered that he was the man with the red-haired wench who had spit on her at the wharf. He continued talking to reassure her. "I am surprised that you did not run also. Is this the first time you have seen an Indian?" He crooked his elbow for her to take his arm.

Pretending not to see his arm, she fell into step beside him, the Indian following a few paces behind. She knew it was improper for her to be walking with him without an appropriate chaperone, but it seemed preferable to walking back alone and contending with the possibility of more Indians and over-eager bachelors. She finally answered his question, "*Oui, Monsieur,* he is the first Indian I have seen except in pictures, and he is unlike any picture I have seen. He is your servant then and not a wild Natchez?"

"*Non,* he is a Choctaw. They have usually been friendly to the French. They are not as dangerous as the Natchez, nor as smart or as brave unfortunately." His hand brushed her elbow as if to steady her over the boards laid down in the muddy streets.

Madeleine walked with perfect balance, needing no steadying. He watched her admiringly.

"*Monsieur*, why did you call him such an insulting name, 'Lying Boy'?"

Jacques laughed again at her concern for his servant's feelings. "That is the only identity with meaning for him. He would be insulted if I called him anything else. It was his tribe that gave him the name, not I."

"*Mais, pourquoi?*"

"It seems that he has always liked to tell stories, even as a boy. If the truth were dull, he would embellish it to make it more interesting or funnier. But the Choctaws' one virtue is honesty; they hate liars. So they expelled him from the tribe."

"How cruel! And just for having a little imagination! Couldn't they have called him Story Teller? Well, at least he fits in with the French, *n'est-ce pas*?" Jacques smiled; he liked her dry wit.

"How did he become your servant?"

Jacques wondered as he answered her how she managed to be so appealing without flirting the way other French girls did. "My platoon and I found him a few miles out of New Orleans, half-starved and grieving for lack of companionship. We took him in and I made him my personal servant. To keep him happy, I let him play a joke on me now and then."

"You have no problem with his lying then?"

"*Non*, he never lies about anything important. He simply likes to weave preposterous stories. I enjoy them. It is always obvious when he is inventing something for his amusement, or for mine."

Madeleine smiled, a rarity in her lovely but often remote face. Jacques was even more charmed by her, thinking that she should definitely smile more often. They walked in companionable silence for a while. As if to fill that silence, the Indian walking behind them started to hum a French tune in a surprisingly musical voice. Jacques noted Madeleine's surprise and explained: "The name Choctaw means 'charming voice.' Most of them can sing beautifully. I have heard that they can be taught to play musical instruments."

"Interesting," commented Madeleine.

Then Jacques stopped abruptly, turned to her, and said urgently, "*Mademoiselle*, we are almost to the convent. I must ask you, have you consented to any of the numerous offers of marriage I know you must have gotten?"

Madeleine saw that indeed they were only a few steps from the Bienville Hotel, where interested faces were look-ing out the windows of both stories in the temporary con-vent. She stopped smiling, moved a little farther away from him, and answered simply, "*Non, Monsieur.*" She started for the gate.

He commented approvingly, "So you are discriminat-ing as well as lovely and brave. My troop was called to in-vestigate what turned out to be another false alarm about the Natchez the day after your arrival. Otherwise I would have paid you a call to see how you were."

Madeleine thought his statement was a little noncom-mittal. Did this mean he was interested in her as a wife? He must have known that she as well as the other *casquette* girls came to Louisiana to get married. Also, she was not sure she liked his taking for granted that she would have remembered him from that one brief encoun-ter at the *quai*. She wondered too what his connection to the red-haired woman was. Now at the doorsteps of the convent, she turned to him and said rather coldly, "That would have been extremely gracious of you, as you have been in escorting me home. *Merci beaucoup.*"

He held out his hand as if to keep her a moment longer. "Would it displease you if I called on you to get better acquainted?"

"The other girls and I receive visitors every afternoon. I am sure we would all be happy to see you."

Jacques was surprised and not a little intrigued at her cool manner. He was accustomed to women, few as they were here, fawning over him because of his looks and his aristocratic name. "*Au revoir* for now, *Mademoiselle.*"

Madeleine nodded and went inside to be bombarded by questions from fifty-nine curious girls.

Chapter 12

Madeleine sat alone in front of the fireplace at the Bienville Hotel in a rare moment of inactivity and solitude for her. Over four months had passed since she had arrived in New Orleans. She was awaiting the New Year, 1729, and wondering what it held for her. All of the *casquette* girls except for her were now married. Suzanne had married one of the suitors Madeleine rejected, the wealthy merchant, Jean Claude Chauvin. Though Madeleine had congratulated them warmly and wished them well, they both had trouble not showing their resentment toward her—he for being rejected, she for not being her husband's first choice. The Chauvins moved to one of the few nice residences in New Orleans, a fact that Suzanne did not often let the other *casquette* girls forget.

Most of the other girls married well, young French officers or employees of the Company. The plain sisters, Simone and Delphine, having fewer choices, broke precedent and married British colonists. Simone married Hank Davis, the Kentuckian who worked as a guide now. Delphine married a friend of his who looked very much like him. The four had left town the day after the big Christmas wedding to live on the men's homesteads— Simone and Hank to Biloxi and Delphine and Hank's friend to Fort Rosalie. Madeleine thought the two sisters were relieved to leave New Orleans, for it was considered a disgrace to marry English frontiersmen, believed to be uncivilized by the French. She had felt a definite chill in the air whenever Simone's and Delphine's suitors came into the room.

Before Jacques Bouligny left on his last foray into Natchez Indian country, he had asked Madeleine to wait for him even though he still had made no outright proposal. That was three months ago. The other girls thought she was a fool to wait, though they all admitted his looks and background made him the most desirable of all their suitors. His family was almost as illustrious as the de Mandevilles. Before Suzanne accepted Chauvin, she had used all her wiles to attract Jacques's attention, but he seemed to prefer the cool dignity of Madeleine. Suzanne suggested spitefully to Simone, not in Madeleine's hearing, that he must prefer the de Mandeville name.

Madeleine wondered herself if she were being foolish. She admired Jacques and considered herself fortunate to be chosen by him, if his asking her to wait indeed meant being chosen. She had not been alone with him since their walk from the levee, but he had kept his promise to visit her during those hours allowed by the nuns, becoming a regular visitor who charmed all the women with his gallantry, wit, and gracious manners. Madeleine had to concentrate hard to avoid giving her true background away. She knew he was an authentic nobleman and one mistake could reveal her humble origins. She learned the trick of pretending she was the Countess de Mandeville. The cooler and more distant she was the warmer Jacques became. As a result of her playing a role and their lack of privacy, they knew each other no better than that day he walked her home from the levee.

The past four months for Madeleine had been quiet but busy. Most of her suitors had given up, feeling they had little chance because of the handsome, sought-after Lieutenant Bouligny courting her. But there was another, more troubling, reason besides Jacques's charm and eligibility that had prompted many of Madeleine's other suitors to give up courting her. Whenever Jacques came to call, Madeleine noticed that other officers, even those of comparable rank, treated him with an edgy, grudging sort of respect, their manner being partly one of fear, she thought. Later, from other girls but never from Jacques himself, she learned the reasons for this attitude—his explosive temper in any sort of argument and his intimidating skill with word and sword. It seemed, she admitted woefully to herself, that Jacques Bouligny was quick to accept any challenge and quite capable of backing it up.

To fill her time while she waited for Jacques to return, she helped the nuns care for the bedridden in the hospital. Though Jacques had murmured some disapproval of her working there with mostly wounded soldiers or victims of drunken brawls, she enjoyed being useful. The Ursuline nuns began to think of her as almost one of them, and the patients were in awe of this cool beauty who wiped their brows and performed the most menial tasks with calm efficiency.

Madeleine also helped with the school for young ladies that the nuns ran at the temporary convent. She soon found that she had educated herself more thoroughly than most of these young ladies had been taught. She sat in on the Sisters' classes and picked up even more knowledge. The Sisters soon found that she was able to conduct a class herself. She was especially compassionate toward the Negro and Indian girls who were allowed to come to the school to learn sewing, catechism, and their letters. Madeleine even picked up a few Choctaw words.

Madeleine sighed and moved closer to the fire. Winter in New Orleans was as cold as the summer was hot. The humidity from the river and the Gulf turned into an icy wet cold that penetrated clothes and walls and chilled the bones. At least people were not plagued by mosquitoes in the wintertime. She had grown fond of this spacious hotel where the nuns were quartered until their convent was finished. Now that the other *casquette* girls were gone, the two-story building seemed large with only Madeleine, the ten nuns, and the four servants who were left.

Madeleine longed to be in her own home. She thought about the fact that she had never lived in her own home. Even her parents' small shack had been owned by the de Mandevilles. This was the first time she had ever had a bedroom to herself. She leaned back in her chair, closed her eyes, and dreamed of Jacques and her in their own home, perhaps on Chartres Street below the cathedral. For a moment Captain Beauchamp's strong bearded face took the place of Jacques' clean-shaven one, but only for a moment. She shook off the image and returned to her daydream about Jacques, hoping it would have a better chance of becoming a reality.

She ached to be in control of her own destiny. She envied the other *casquette* girls when she visited them. Now that they were married, they no longer had to be chaperoned wherever they went. They decided how they would fill their days, and most had servants to take care of unpleasant tasks like scrubbing floors and cooking meals, both of which Madeleine sometimes helped the nuns do, the four servants not being enough to clean the nuns' living quarters in addition to the school, orphanage, and hospital.

Most of the girls who stayed in or near New Orleans saw each other often. They felt a bond with each other, but they also seemed to have an unspoken agreement that it was in their best interests to set themselves apart. After all, they had been chosen for their virtue and respectability and already were becoming social leaders. They tried to exercise the calming, settling effect on the primitive, rowdy little town that Governor Bienville had hoped for.

As the clock struck midnight, Madeleine walked to the window and opened the shutters braving the cold air for a moment. She listened to the loud sounds of merriment greeting the New Year and did not regret that she had turned down all invitations to parties and celebrations. She watched the sleet and rainfall, a little hazy through the thin linen stretched over the window frame. The glassless windows were another reminder that she was far from what she considered civilization. She wondered how long it would be before luxuries like glass could be shipped here without being broken.

Trying to avoid thinking of ships, she closed the shutters and returned to the fire. She felt guilty for pitying herself when she knew Jacques might be out in this weather. He might even be in danger. The whole town seemed to be afraid that the Natchez might attack anywhere at any moment. She thought with wry amusement that their apprehension did not cause them to cancel any parties tonight. The French could always find something to celebrate.

Madeleine tried to shake her feeling of loneliness. She wished she had joined the nuns at the hospital. They anticipated a busy night, taking care of many New Year's Eve revelers. There were always fights and knifings in the cabaret district. The nuns wanted to protect her and insisted that she stay at the convent, but at least she would have been too busy to feel so alone if she had been at the hospital. Maybe soon, she thought, I will have a family and a home of my own to care for.

Well, there is no point in brooding. I might as well go to bed. Madeleine lit a candle from the lamp and blew out the lamp. Just as she started to bank the fire, she heard a soft knock at the door. She opened it to a dripping, half-frozen Jacques. She was both delighted and alarmed to see him at this hour. For decorum's sake, she did not throw open the door for him.

"Madeleine, *ma cherie*, I was on my way to my barracks when I saw you at the window. I have just returned from duty upriver and I had to see you. Forgive me. It has been so long I could not wait till morning."

She hesitated a moment, then said, "I am happy to see you too. Come in and warm yourself for a moment; then you must go. The sisters are all at the hospital, but I don't know when some will return." She pulled her shawl around her white cotton nightdress for modesty, but not before Jacques had gotten a glimpse of her lovely, slender body through the soft, thin material.

Impulsively he embraced her, his wet clothes dampening her nightdress. She could feel his hardness against her. He kissed her hungrily and pulled her body even closer. Madeleine began to feel as if she were being devoured and pulled away. At first he would not let her go, but she pleaded, "Please, Jacques. I cannot allow you to do this. *Please!*"

As he released her, she lost her grip on her shawl for a moment. Her small firm breasts were outlined clearly through the damp material clinging to them. He reached out toward her again, his eyes glittering in passion. Madeleine quickly stepped back and gathered the shawl once more about her.

"Forgive me," he said. "It has been so long since I saw you, but I have thought of you constantly. I was afraid you would be married by now. When I saw you in the convent window, I knew I had not lost you. Then, when I saw you so lovely in your nightgown, as you will be when you are my wife, I felt that you were already mine."

Madeleine was in a turmoil, her heart racing from their embrace. She didn't know if she felt fear or excitement. She had felt different in Captain Beauchamp's arms—safer, protected perhaps. But Jacques' embrace had thrilled her in a stranger, less comforting way. For the first time he looked a little uncivilized to her, his curly black hair wet and in disarray, his face flushed.

"But this is not suitable. We are not betrothed, and we are unchaperoned. I have not heard from you in over three months, and now you talk about marriage and treat me as if I am already your wife. You have not asked me if that is what I wish."

Jacques immediately became the perfect gentleman again, even looking at her with new respect. "Of course, you are right. I was overcome with excitement at seeing you. My men and I have been guarding the river north of New Orleans. The Chickasaws have been ambushing passengers coming downriver."

Madeleine, still flustered from his kiss, tried to get her mind on what he was saying. "But I thought it was the Natchez Indians that were causing trouble."

"It is true that we expect trouble from the Natchez because of that idiot Etcheparre who is in charge of Fort Rosalie, but the Chickasaws have always hated the French. The British encourage them to be a constant problem."

"But you are all right? You must have been in danger."

Jacques nodded yes and said, "Madeleine, I did not come here to talk about Indians." He reached in his pocket and pulled out a small velvet bag from which he took a heavy gold ring engraved with delicate flowers. "My beautiful Madeleine, did you doubt my intentions? Please take this ring and keep it as proof of my intentions until we can be married. It was my grandmother's; now it is yours. Since I was her favorite, she left it to me to give to my wife. I think she wanted to compensate for my having such a small inheritance as a younger son. I am not a wealthy man because of being the youngest in my family."

A moment passed in silence. Jacques watched carefully for any reaction to this information that he was poor. When Madeleine gave none, he felt safe to continue, "I did not make our betrothal official because I wanted to make sure I returned safely. It has been my intention all along to join the de Mandeville and the Bouligny names."

Madeleine felt a little apprehension at this statement—and no small amount of shame, as it partially echoed her own motives. "Is this to be a merger then?"

"My dear, I worship you. You are the perfect woman. I never dreamed I would find someone with all your qualities. You have beauty, virtue, and a good name. Did I not tell you this that first day when you arrived?" He asked this last question hiding a smile.

Madeleine took the ring in her hand and felt its substantial weight. She was happy that he had finally declared himself but felt something was missing. Something more than concern for his safety must have kept him from speaking out. After all, as long as he remained a French soldier, he would be in some danger.

"Jacques, do you think you will find it difficult to give up being a bachelor?"

Jacques looked at her as if his pet dog had bitten him. "Why do you ask that? I would not ask you to marry me if I minded giving up my life as a bachelor."

Madeleine worded her reply carefully, aware that she was treading in dangerous waters. "Some men enjoy their freedom. They become accustomed to having no obligations."

Jacques was equally cautious. "Is there some particular aspect of my life you are concerned about?"

Madeleine decided to be frank. "The red-haired woman standing close to you on the day of my arrival, the one who insulted me and spit on me—I believe her name is Marie—what does she mean to you?"

Jacques was startled by her direct question. "Ah, she was my ah—that is, we were very close for a time. Well, not *really* close. There have never been many women in

New Orleans. Especially not decent women."

"Then Marie is not a decent woman? And she is your mistress? Do you intend to keep her as your mistress?"

Jacques tried to hide his shock at her questions. Most women ignored matters such as mistresses. "It is true that she was my, ah, mistress, but I stopped seeing her after that day when I ran into you at the levee." He made a vow to himself to go directly to Marie after leaving to make that statement into the truth.

He took her hand and closed it around the ring. "Please believe me, Madeleine, I would not need a mistress if I were married to you. A man gets very lonely here, but you would fill all my needs."

"Perhaps I am not all I seem. I am not sure I can be all you think I am."

Jacques smiled confidently. "I am sure enough for both of us. You have not answered me. Will you keep the ring and become my wife?"

Madeleine too smiled, putting her doubts out of her mind. "*Oui*, I am proud to become your wife."

Jacques started to pull her toward him again. "*Ma cherie*, you have made me the happiest man in New Orleans."

This time Madeleine pulled gently out of his arms. "Now you must go or your fiancée's reputation for virtue will be ruined."

After Madeleine closed the door on a reluctant Jacques, she breathed a deep sigh and looked at the ring in her hand. At last, she thought, my future is settled. I will have a home and family of my own. He is poor, but we can acquire money with hard work. Resolutely, she ignored the few doubts that nagged at her and went to bed.

Jacques too went to bed soon after that conversation with his fiancée, but he did not go to bed alone. He snuggled next to the soft, full body of Marie, both satiated from lovemaking, and listened to the last sounds of the New Year's revelers. He thought of how difficult it was going to be to give up his freedom as a bachelor, but he knew Madeleine was a prize well worth the sacrifice.

As the light of dawn awakened Marie too, he took her face gently in his hands and told her about his coming marriage to Madeleine. Marie came alive as suddenly and explosively as the fireworks outside their window on Burgundy Street. Her red hair seemed to crackle as she yelled at him, "You bastard, you promised to marry me! You are the only man I've taken to my bed since I met you."

"Calm down, my pet. We all say things in the heat of passion that we don't really mean. We can't be held accountable for being carried away at the moment. A Bouligny simply cannot marry a, uh, barmaid."

"A pox on you and the Bouligny name! A barmaid was good enough for you before those *casquette* girls came to New Orleans." She jumped up from bed, her bare flesh quivering in the cold, and continued to shout, "Of all the women to choose—that thin, prissy stick of wood, Madeleine de Mandeville. You'll catch your death of cold in her bed."

Jacques tried to placate her. "Marie, no woman could satisfy me after you. After I've been married for a while, perhaps we can resume our friendship."

Marie became so incensed at these words she ripped the bedcoverings from the bed, throwing him on the floor and causing him to scramble for his clothes. "I'll be damned if I will take up the slack for that bitch and do her job for her. A pox on you both! Get the hell out of my room! Get out!"

Jacques bid her a hasty *adieu* as he hurried out the door only to find a small crowd of amused party-goers witnessing their farewell. They roared in laughter when Marie appeared in the doorway shaking her fist, anger juggling her large breasts in tandem, and yelled, "You'll be sorry for this, you bastard! I won't always be a barmaid. I'll get even with you if it takes the rest of my life!"

Jacques assumed a jaunty manner, said something to the crowd about a woman scorned, and walked away whistling.

Chapter 13

Madeleine and Jacques walked out of the church into the bright afternoon sunlight of a cold February day—as man and wife. They strode smiling, arm in arm, through a gauntlet of well-wishers, all of whom exclaimed at what an extraordinarily handsome couple they made, both tall, slim, proudly erect, and dark-haired. They seemed too elegant for the frontier life they must lead.

Madeleine was breathtaking in her freshly cleaned, white wool dress with the de Mandeville brooch at her neck. She wore her unpowdered hair in loose waves and coils instead of the usual severe twist. Jacques looked dapper beside her in his new captain's uniform with its polished gold stripes, representing a promotion as a result of his new status as a responsible married man.

Madeleine had become something of a celebrity in the town, this last *casquette* girl to marry. The Ursuline nuns, the other *casquette* girls—as they were still called—and their husbands, the officers and Company officials, all turned out to see the alliance between the most attractive, best connected couple in town. The invited guests, all the best families, filing out of church behind the couple were surprised to see so many of what they considered riff-raff—orphans and former patients of Madeleine's.

Governor Perier demonstrated his approval of the marriage by giving a wedding reception, so all the guests made a procession to his elegant home on the corner of Conti and Royal Streets. There they drank champagne, ate wild game and pastries, and danced. By midnight, Madeleine was worried about what was ahead for her. She was exhausted by dancing, it seemed to her, with every man at the party. She finally prevailed upon Jacques to leave, in spite of many laughing, pointed remarks about the bride being more eager than the groom. Most were careful not to be too crude. They did not want to offend the proud, reserved Madeleine, by whom they were more than a little awed, or the hot-tempered Jacques. The couple left amid a flurry of goodbyes and Godspeeds. They were like an enchanted couple, seemingly more privileged with their beauty and grace than anyone else. Even Suzanne, now pregnant with her first child, admitted grudgingly that they made an attractive pair.

Carrying a lantern to light the way, Madeleine and Jacques walked hand in hand the short distance to Dauphine Street where Jacques had secured a room for them with a respectable family, the Parraults, who had thoughtfully arranged to spend the evening with neighbors. When, shivering from the cold and perhaps from nervousness, they arrived at the small frame house with the even smaller yard, Jacques unlocked the door to the back entrance leading to their room.

"Well, here we are," he said uneasily and guided her through a short hallway, filled with family pictures of people Madeleine did not know and the odor of unaired rooms, to a small dark room crowded with furniture too large for it.

Madeleine looked around in a daze and wanted to run back to the familiar safety of the convent. She wished she could run all the way back to France and the de Mandeville home. Was it for this she had traveled so far? This cheaply furnished room to share with a stranger? What had she done? It would have been better to have stayed with the nuns and worked in the hospital and the school, until she could repay her passage money to the Company.

Jacques turned the lamp up and hung it on the wall. The room looked even shabbier then to Madeleine. She wondered if the Parraults had stored their extra furniture in the room. Taking up most of the space was a painted iron bedstead with a feather mattress covered by a quilt not quite large enough to cover the mattress. Jacques put his hat on a chipped pine armoire. Madeleine opened a drawer and was relieved to see the some of the contents of her *casquette* that Jacques had moved from the convent early that morning, a time that seemed a year ago.

Jacques watched her carefully and noticed how quiet she was. "I know it is not as elegant as you are accustomed to." Madeleine smiled at this and became reconciled to the room, thinking that what she had been accustomed to was even worse.

"I had to use my pay for some unforeseen expenses this month," he said. "And I don't get my stipend from my family until the *les Belles Soeurs* arrives again. I hope you can manage with these humble quarters temporarily."

Madeleine tried to reassure him. "This will be fine, Jacques. We won't need much room at first. And I will have the opportunity to get acquainted with another family."

"*Oui*, I thought your being with the Parraults would keep you from being so lonely when I am away."

Madeleine thought that she would like being alone in her own home above all things, but she merely said, "How thoughtful of you."

Jacques seemed relieved then. Though he was already a little unsteady on his feet, he asked, "Well, how about a glass of wine first?"

Madeleine wondered about his use of the word *first*. Was his mind then so much on what was *second*? "That would be very nice." To avoid looking at him, she started to fold her few clothes in the chifforobe. She could not help but notice the array of expensive looking clothes Jacques had. Could these have been his "unforeseen expenses"? She immediately felt guilty. How could she begin her marriage being so critical? Was she impossibly mean-spirited and suspicious? Was it not his elegance that attracted her to him? That and the Bouligny name?

She crossed the room and sat beside Jacques on a small overstuffed couch. Jacques gave her a glass of wine and lifted his glass. "To the ideal woman and the ideal marriage." They softly clicked glasses and sipped.

"Madeleine, it is too cold to stay up. I think we will get warm only in bed." He tried to hide the eagerness in his voice. "Perhaps you would like to change behind this screen." He got a folded screen leaning against the wall and set it up for her in the corner of the room.

Madeleine wished they had talked a little longer until

she felt more relaxed with him. She was relieved to notice that he at least waited politely until she was behind the screen before he started to undress. She disrobed slowly in spite of the cold, prolonging the minutes before she would have to join him in bed.

Jacques removed his clothes quickly and sank into the feather bed, covering his slender, wiry body with the blanket and quilt. He watched the screen with anticipation, then noticed that he could see his new wife's reflection in a smoky mirror on the wall. She had removed her stays and petticoat and was slipping out of her shift. Her boyishly slim body enchanted him, so different from the overblown whores like Marie and Indian women he had bedded. He throbbed with excitement. He could hardly wait to possess this cool beauty. He had to force himself to wait for her. He wanted to tear down the screen and grab that white body with its high firm breasts and long tapering waist.

Madeleine quickly slipped on her thin linen nightgown with fine lace around the yoke. As she stepped from behind the screen, she saw Jacques' reflection in the mirror, his eyes glittering with lust and realized he had been watching her as she had undressed. She felt a momentary flash of anger at this invasion of her privacy; then she stifled it. After all, they were married now. She must get used to the idea that her body belonged to him and that her most personal habits would no longer be private. She could no longer think of herself as a separate person.

Madeleine walked over to the bed and let down her hair. Jacques became even more aroused as he saw the black, shining cascade of hair fall nearly to her waist, completely covering her shoulders and breasts. He could restrain himself no longer. He pulled her eagerly into bed and pressed his body against hers. Madeleine tentatively reached up her hand and touched his face. She longed to be held and kissed gently until her fears were gone.

Jacques's needs were quite different. He was consumed by his lust. He wrapped her hair around his hands and kissed her passionately, forcing her mouth open with his tongue. Madeleine was shocked and tried to pull away, never having been kissed this way. Then he abruptly pulled up her gown and explored her body, now stiff with fear. Not seeming to be surprised at her lack of response, he climbed on top of her and pushed his way into her unprepared body. Madeleine pressed her mouth against his shoulder to keep from screaming in pain. Fortunately, her agony was brief. His driving body went into a spasm and collapsed on hers, then completely relaxed.

Madeleine lay under him in a state of shock until he went quickly to sleep and she was able to move from under him and pull down her gown. She buried her head in the crook of her arm to stifle her sobs. She thought with irony that being seen naked in the mirror was a small invasion of privacy compared to this—this violation of her body. Did she really just tell herself that her body belonged to her husband? Could she possibly get used to this? How did other married women manage? She remembered what Suzanne had said on the ship about pitying Madeleine's husband on their wedding night. Pity her husband indeed!

Chapter 14

Somehow Madeleine did endure her marriage and the winter. She did not grow to enjoy her brief couplings with Jacques, but at least they became less painful. Jacques seemed to think her lack of enthusiasm was only proper for a lady and did not complain. She wondered if he noticed.

She grew to know him much better, perhaps better than she wished in that small, cramped room. Much of what she learned she did not like. For one thing, she found that his "unforeseen expenses" usually involved gambling, another passion of his. He seemed to be two people: by day, a sober, industrious soldier with a strong sense of propriety and, by night, a hard-drinking, gambling, passionate man without a care for the honor of his name or for his wife.

He was frequently gone for weeks at a time, and when he returned he was often gone at night. Though he secretly approved of Madeleine's lack of interest in parties and frivolous activities, this left them little to talk about. Madeleine was torn between feeling abandoned and feeling relieved to be left alone so much. Accustomed to work, she kept busy. Her first project was to make their room more livable. She soon realized that it would not be as temporary as Jacques had at first suggested.

After giving the room a thorough cleaning and airing, she stored the heavy chifforobe, containing Jacques' less frequently worn clothes, in the Parraults' attic. The armoire was sufficient for their needs, and the loss of the unneeded piece of furniture gave them space to walk around. She refinished the armoire and mended the splits in the sofa. In a frenzy of activity and in record time, she made a coverlet that properly fit the bed and matching curtains for the small window. She charged the material at the Chauvin's store, though it made her uneasy to owe Suzanne's husband money. Jacques did not give her any money but had told her to charge necessities. She found small paintings of Jacques' family and hung them on the walls, trying not to feel like an imposter borrowing his family. Now at least she had made the one small room into a haven when he was away.

Madeleine spent much of her time at the convent volunteering to help in the school. At first she continued to help at the hospital; but, when Jacques found out, he became livid with rage and forbade her to work there. She saw his famous temper for the first time. As she was not the type to wheedle and beg, she had no choice but to give in. After all, a husband's word, especially a Frenchman's, was law. No virtuous wife would dare disobey him. Occasionally she guiltily fantasized about being married to

Captain Beauchamp. She doubted that, even sailing for months at a time, he would leave her alone more that Jacques did.

She spent more time with Mrs. Parrault and her two small children than she wished. Since Robert Parrault was a lieutenant in the French army, he was gone almost as often as Jacques was, so the two women were left alone together a great deal of time. Madeleine found Anne Parrault to be fun-loving and goodhearted, but not a stimulating conversationalist. She helped her with her housework and children, since the Parraults had no servant. In return for this work, she and Jacques were not charged for their food. When Anne let it slip that Jacques was behind on the rent, Madeleine was so embarrassed she helped out even more.

Lying Boy also adjusted to the new household. The Parraults were leery of having an Indian under their roof when Jacques first asked that he be allowed to move in. After some hesitation, they insulated the lean-to at the back of the house for him. They soon realized that he was harmless and would not butcher them in their sleep. He remained Jacques's personal servant and went wherever Jacques went. The women could count on him only to run a few errands. He pretended not to understand their instructions on any chore he did not want to do, even though he could understand French quite well and though Madeleine was becoming more proficient in Choctaw. He was good at amusing the children because he was so close to being a child himself. He told them stories in half Choctaw and half French and made them laugh until they rolled on the floor in delight. At first the women thought they could not understand much of what he said. They thought the children must be laughing at his gestures and antics as he told his stories; but, when they heard the kids talking to each other in broken Choctaw, they changed their minds.

Madeleine grew fond of Lying Boy even though he created more work when he was around as he had to be fed too. And he refused to clean his lean-to; he preferred it dirty. Jacques and Anne tried to persuade Madeleine to leave it as it was, but she could not bear dirt or disorder around her. So, whenever the men left, she held her nose and cleaned the lean-to. In the beginning Lying Boy seemed jealous of her but he grew to respect her. She never laughed at his stories, but he seemed to know she could be depended on completely. Lying Boy gave Madeleine a small sense of family. He belonged to them. He was not borrowed or rented.

Whenever she could, Madeleine escaped to her room to read. She continued to borrow from the nuns' library. She also resumed her long walks and learned to love New Orleans and the land surrounding it. She often walked along the levee and watched the boats come in. Occasionally a pirogue would bring sailors from a ship docked at La Balize, but never from *les Belles Soeurs*. On Saturday nights the Germans would float their produce down the river and sell it on Sunday morning. Madeleine would join Mrs. Parrault and the other women in choosing fresh vegetables and fruit for the week. She got to know a particularly industrious German family, the Muellers, who were the first to arrive and the last to leave. They stocked the finest vegetables but struck the hardest bargain. When they saw in Madeleine someone of like mind, they began to save their freshest produce for her. They respected her sure eye for the best quality. She found that she remembered most of the recipes she had learned from the de Mandeville chef and prepared delicious meals for the Parraults and for Jacques when he was home.

Madeleine was alarmed that there was still much talk in the town about Indian problems. Some planters had moved their families to town temporarily for fear of not being able to protect them. Governor Perier, just as Bienville had before him, requested more troops to protect the area, but to no avail. Jacques and his men continued to be overworked.

One afternoon Madeleine and Mrs. Parrault were shelling peas for the evening meal when they heard a loud commotion. They ran outside and saw a woman running down the street screaming that Indians were killing all the men, women and children in Bayou St. John where she was from. Governor Perier called a general alarm. Women and children were taken to the church and aboard boats on the river. Men armed themselves and gathered in the *Place d'Arms.*

Two hours later there had been no sign of an attack. Madeleine, who had taken the woman sounding the alarm to the convent, calmed her down and questioned her more thoroughly. She found that the woman had drunk too much *tafia*, a low-grade rum made from cheap molasses. Because of the general hysteria about Indians, she had built a peaceful visit by some friendly Indians way out of proportion. When the other people of New Orleans heard the truth, they shrugged their shoulders and turned the occasion into a party. They drank and danced and celebrated the Indians not attacking. They enjoyed themselves so much that nobody criticized the woman for alarming the town unnecessarily.

Madeleine found that these diversions were not enough for her. Now that spring was here, she was restless. Work, school, and Jacques's infrequent visits did not fill her life. Jacques kept telling her that she would soon have a baby to keep her busy, but so far she was not *enceinte*. She wondered how they would pay to feed and clothe a child if she had one. She felt her life was stalled, that things were not changing, not improving. She was dissatisfied living in someone else's house. She still wanted her own home; but, whenever she mentioned it to Jacques, he became angry.

He continued to spend many of his nights gambling and drinking, and she was beginning to wonder if he were also seeing other women. Shortly after their own marriage, she heard that Marie had married Michael O'Brien, the red-haired Company clerk who sailed with the *casquette* girls on *les Belles Soeurs* and who had been so smitten with Madeleine that he had mistakenly given her the name de Mandeville. Suzanne had delighted in telling Madeleine that Marie and Michael had pooled their earnings and bought the bar Marie had worked in. Suzanne particularly relished telling her that Marie was pregnant. Suzanne, now large with child herself, kept Madeleine informed of all the *casquette* girls' progress, especially their pregnancies.

"When are you going to start a family, Madeleine? Maybe you are doing something wrong in bed."

"What can I do right, Suzanne? Perhaps you can advise me since you have had so much practice."

Suzanne implied so often that Madeleine was deficient she began wonder herself what she was doing wrong. Would she ever belong anywhere?

Madeleine watched the town grow and prosper. As she watched the other *casquette* girls make homes and start families, she became envious and more frustrated. She despaired that Jacques would ever change and save enough money to buy a home or property. The enchanted couple no longer seemed so lucky.

Chapter 15

Spring made the most hardened cynic an admirer of New Orleans, for nature seemed to strain itself to dress the city in an extravagant display of semitropical growth. The air, sometimes humidly heavy, bore the scent of jasmine and magnolia, while the freshly washed sunshine sparkled from the pastels of dogwood and columbine. Wild mint and cultivated tobacco offered a spicy, sharper odor of contrast, and even the bothersome weeds growing in the moist delta soil offered a heavy green backdrop for the vivid splashes of color exploding everywhere. The transplanted Europeans felt that maybe this land, which had seemed so forbidding at first, really was a corner of paradise.

Madeleine continued to see growth and prosperity all around her. Every day she saw more ships, boats, rafts, and barges carrying cargoes as varied as the people bringing them—furs and lumber and foodstuffs of all sorts.

Merchants were busy putting up retail shops and ware-houses, while most everybody else, regardless of occupation, seemed to be building, expanding, or refining a house or a shanty to live in. All the while, she noted sadly, the mud and the dust, alternating for dominance, clung to the shoes and boots of all, for the streets remained little more than well-worn paths of dirt. Even so, she thrilled to the energetic spirit of expansion that was rapidly changing the appearance of New Orleans.

Madeleine and Anne Parrault joined the recent craze of growing tobacco by planting some in the Parraults' small back yard. They persuaded Lying Boy to do some of the physical work, but Madeleine did most of it herself. The Company, which had formerly been less than generous in sending slaves to its Louisiana colony, suddenly promised slaves to anyone growing tobacco. Madeleine and Anne laughed to see tobacco planted in even smaller yards than theirs. Anne actually had little hope of getting a slave, but she said she would need two after Madeleine moved out and into her own home, an event that Madeleine was beginning to doubt would ever occur.

Jacques was surprised that Madeleine knew anything about planting. She nervously told him her old lie about helping to supervise the gardens on the de Mandeville country estate. He was beginning to believe she could indeed do anything. He had stopped teasing her about being the ideal woman because he felt that her competence in so many areas had become formidable. The two had not grown any closer. Madeleine found it harder and harder to respect and obey this man who gambled away most of their money and used her body at night as if she were a chamber pot.

113

Though Jacques took Madeleine for granted and expected her to be the perfect wife at all times, he sensed there were parts of her that she withheld. She did not completely belong to him. She was not open and loving and flirtatious as his friends' wives were. She never chattered. When they were alone in their room, she preferred reading to talking. He began to be a little in awe of her and sought out women with whom he felt more comfortable.

Another problem was Jacques's gambling; he seemed to lose more than he won. On the rare occasions when Madeleine was able to persuade him to give her his winnings to save, he soon demanded them back. He would tell her that they would be able to buy their own home quicker if he used the money for a stake and won big. This particularly frustrated her because it hurt her pride to ask for the money to begin with. She wished that she could be like Suzanne or even Anne, who could teasingly wheedle money out of their men. She simply did not have the light touch. Every time she had to ask for something she stiffened up and the request came out like a cold demand.

She soon learned, when Jacques gave her his winnings, to immediately spend the money on things they would need for their home, if they ever got one. Thus, she soon had a small stock of china, linens, and even a few pieces of furniture stored in the Parraults' attic. Of course, when Jacques realized she was spending the money on things so she would not have it to return it to him for gambling, he stopped giving it to her to keep.

One benefit did come out of the gambling. One night Jacques and Lying Boy came home from Jacques's game of faro, and Jacques shook Madeleine awake. He insisted she wrap up and come into the hallway where she could see a grinning Lying Boy through the open door. At first thinking it was a drunken prank, she resisted; but, when she heard another voice, a feminine one, she got up to investigate. Standing beside a delighted looking Lying Boy was a sturdy, buxom Indian woman giggling shyly behind her hand. "Madeleine, meet your new lady's maid extraordinaire and Lying Boy's companion, Laughing Girl."

Madeleine simply stared at the self-satisfied, half-drunken trio. "Where in name of *le bon Dieu* did you get her? Is not one Indian we can barely feed enough?"

"I won her from a trapper in a faro game."

"Well, you can give her back to the trapper," she said indignantly. "There is no room for her here. Besides, it is not right to wager a human being in a poker game."

Jacques replied, "Would it be more ethical to buy her like a slave, as the Parraults intend to do because of your tobacco venture?"

When Madeleine had no answer for this, he continued. "I can't give her back. She doesn't want to go back. The trapper beat her. Look!" He pulled down the back of Laughing Girl's dress, revealing some old scars and several new red welts. Laughing Girl giggled happily at the attention.

Madeleine's expression softened with pity. Jacques could see that she was beginning to give in and pushed relentlessly on. "Another reason I can't let her go is that Laughing Boy would probably leave too. He has developed a strong attachment to her. She laughs at all his stories."

"His leaving might not be the worst thing that could happen," she replied tartly, not meaning it.

The two Indians responded by laughing uproariously, holding on to each other for support. Although Laughing

Girl obviously could not understand a word Madeleine was saying, she had to hold her sides from laughing so hard.

"At least I don't have to ask you how she got her name. No wonder Lying Boy is, as you say, strongly attached to her. She laughs at everything."

When Jacques saw her lips almost soften into a smile, he knew the battle was won. "Then she can stay." Turning to Lying Boy, he told him to show his new friend to the lean-to.

"Absolutely not! I will not be a party to their mating like animals. They must be married first."

Ordinarily Jacques deferred to Madeleine on matters of propriety because she was the model of respectability, but this time he felt she was going too far. "You cannot be serious. A marriage ceremony means nothing to them. They are not Christian. Some say they are only half human anyway."

"How can you say that about Lying Boy, who is perhaps your only real friend? Can you look into their eyes and say they are not as human as we are?" After looking at the two, she almost regretted her question, for the two Indians were leaning on each other with glazed eyes and silly smiles, touched with a bit of idiocy that for the moment crowded out whatever intelligence they possessed.

Jacques merely looked from her to the Indians and raised an eyebrow as if there was no more to be said.

"If a marriage ceremony means nothing to them, it does to me," Madeleine insisted. "In any case I would never be able to convince Anne of this arrangement unless they are married. You will have to sleep with Lying Boy in the lean-to, and Laughing Girl—I hate these names—will sleep on the floor of our room. The first thing tomorrow we will find a priest for them."

"Madeleine, that lean-to is filthy!"

"I am sure you have slept in worse places," she replied pointedly.

Jacques did not want to pursue that point. He decided that, having won the war, he could concede the battle to her. Thus, Laughing Girl became a permanent part of their small household. Luckily, she turned out to be a reliable, hard worker, decreasing the work load for Madeleine and Anne considerably.

Chapter 16

Unfortunately, Laughing Girl—Laff, as the children learned to call her—was the only good thing to come out of Jacques's gambling habit. A few nights after this incident, he came home and again woke up Madeleine. This time the news was not good. He told her he had lost a considerable amount; and, though he hedged on the exact amount, Madeleine knew they were in trouble for he had never before admitted it when he lost.

"I am afraid I had to borrow some money from Chauvin. The next stipend from my family should almost cover it, but I'm afraid we must cut down on expenses for a while."

Madeleine, in despair, wondered what expenses she could possibly cut. They seemed to be going backwards instead of forward. She decided that, the next time the nuns offered her money for her teaching, she would take it. Perhaps she could arrange, through them, to do some sewing without anyone else knowing.

She felt a flash of anger at Jacques. "Perhaps you should cut down on your gambling."

His temples throbbed as they always did when he was angry. "How dare you tell me how to handle my money! You would still be penniless in a convent if you had not married me."

Madeleine knew this was no time to point out that she had received other offers and that she was still penniless *with* him.

When she said nothing more, Jacques began to cool off and talk more calmly. "I have tried to sell my land grant, but nobody wants to buy it. It is too easy to get land cheaply."

Madeleine's eyebrows knitted with incomprehension. "Your what? What did you say about land?"

"I suppose I forgot to tell you. As you know, I first went to Quebec with the French army. As an inducement to get me to settle here, I was given 120 acres with the understanding that it would be put under cultivation."

Madeleine was so stunned she could hardly speak, "We, you, own 120 acres of land and you haven't told me!"

"I didn't think it was important. I am no farmer, and I could not sell it. There is uncultivated land everywhere you look."

Madeleine ignored explanations and tried to pull more information out of him. "Where is this land? What kind of soil is on it? Is there any water for irrigation?" She held her breath waiting for the answers.

Jacques was puzzled at her interest. After all, she was essentially an aristocratic Parisian, despite her stories of amusing herself with the gardens on the de Mandeville country estate. This was peasants' talk. "It is twenty miles north of New Orleans, near the German Coast. I have no idea what kind of soil it is, but I suppose it has water. It fronts the Mississippi. Why the questions? Are you thinking about farming it?" he asked in an amused voice.

Madeleine could hardly contain her excitement. "Exactly! It sounds perfect. If it is near the German Coast, that means the soil must be fertile. *Les Allemandes* produce the best crops of anyone. And if it is really on the river," she breathed in wonder, "we are saved."

"But, Madeleine, of what use is it? We are not farmers. It is one thing to grow a few stalks of tobacco in your back yard, but it is quite another to put 120 acres under cultivation without any slaves to help."

"We don't have to cultivate all 120 acres. At first, we can grow enough food for us and the Parraults to eat, then perhaps enough to sell. After that, we can farm all 120 acres."

Jacques looked at her as if she had lost her mind. "I told you, Madeleine, I am not a farmer! Or a peddler of vegetables. I could not grow an onion."

"I can," said Madeleine with more determination than he had ever heard in her voice before. If I can't have a child, I will have another purpose.

Part III.
Magnolia Grove, 1729

Chapter 17

In spring of 1729, Madeleine was happier and more hopeful than she had been since coming to Louisiana. She had finally persuaded Jacques to take her to see the land. It annoyed him a little when she called it *our* land, but she could not help but think of it as hers too.

She, Jacques, Lying Boy, and Laff bounced along in an open carriage borrowed from one of Jacques's fellow officers. It was Madeleine's first real outing. She had packed a picnic basket with cheese, bread, and wine. Following a well-marked trail along the river, it did not take long for them to leave civilization behind. Houses appeared few and far between. Madeleine was reminded of her trip up-river on the barge when she first arrived in Louisiana. As they passed plantations similar to those she had seen before on her first trip to New Orleans, she remembered her desire to live on one. No matter what Jacques said, she believed she now had a chance to make that dream come true.

She looked with fascination as they passed from open fields to woods to swamps to tobacco and rice fields. What a variety of scenery in this Louisiana, she thought. Whatever changes they saw, there remained one constant: lush greenery everywhere. It had a wilder, more untamed look than she was used to in the French countryside. As they rode along the river's edge, she saw rushes growing from the banks right down into the water's edge and huge cypress trees with slimy trunks towering above the low vegetation. At first she was charmed by the moss-covered oaks forming a canopy overhead, but soon the trail became so overgrown they had to stop the buggy so the men could hack away the tangled vines and clumps of palmettos blocking their progress. She caught glimpses of wild animals like wolves and deer and even a few poisonous snakes when the foursome stopped to stretch their legs.

At one point they stopped so Jacques and Lying Boy could shoot two bushy-tailed rodents they called squirrels. They said Laff could skin them and cook them into a stew. Madeleine looked skeptical at this, but Laff nodded and giggled.

After they had traveled for about three hours, the trail became too wild and overgrown for the carriage to get through, so they had to abandon it. They unhitched the two horses; and, without saddles, Jacques and Madeleine rode astride on one, while the Indian couple rode on the other. Finally, they reached a gnarled and knotty oak tree, which Jacques said was the southern boundary for his land.

Madeleine became almost frenzied with excitement. Jacques was amazed at his reserved wife's behavior; he was beginning to realize how much this land meant to her. All he saw was useless wilderness, but evidently she saw something more. Lying Boy and Laff picked up her excitement and were happy to be out in the open spaces again.

One of the first things Madeleine did was check the soil. As they made their way through the underbrush, every few minutes she would stop, dig her hand in the dirt and look at it. At one point she shocked her three traveling companions by tasting the dirt. They could not believe this was their fastidious wife and mistress. Madeleine beamed with happiness. The soil was even better than she had hoped. It was dark, moist, and rich looking. And she noted that moisture was everywhere—that *sine qua non* for all farmers of all lands. The swamps and creeks here apparently kept the soil damp and productive all year round. Near a small swamp farther away from the river, the soil was almost black. She knew it was virgin soil and would easily grow almost anything the weather would permit.

Jacques grew tired and wanted to stop the aimless walking about. "*Ma cherie*, we cannot see the whole 120 acres in one day. Even I have not seen it all. Why do we not rest for a while and have a little wine?"

"*Non*, Jacques, let us go on, please. I want to see the little house you told me about before we stop."

"It is only a rough shack some trappers put up one winter when they stayed here. *Le bon Dieu* knows why they wanted to spend the winter here, miles away from civilization."

"It is beautiful here. Look at the morning glory and the dogwood trees."

Lying Boy looked at Madeleine with new respect. He saw that she had a love of the land that he too shared. He had grown tired of his life in town of drinking and waiting for Jacques in smoky taverns. Laff now took care of his most important need for companionship, and he began to grow hopeful that his mistress might talk Jacques into settling here on this peaceful land.

Jacques scuffed his newly polished boots on a tree stump and began to get irritable. When a tree branch knocked off his hat, he swore: "*Sacre bleu*, Madeleine, I can't remember where the damned shack is."

"There it is, Jacques! Look, I see it! Follow me." In the distance on top of a small hill overlooking the river sat a small ramshackle hut. What delighted Madeleine was that it was set in the middle of a large grove of magnolia trees. Their wide-reaching branches were covered with dark green leaves and waxy white blossoms that gave off a hauntingly sweet aroma and perfumed the air around them. Madeleine pulled one off a branch and put it in her dark hair.

Jacques's energy was renewed at the sight of his unusually animated wife, still fresh looking in her lightweight yellow dress, however faded and darned. "Jacques, we can plant young magnolia trees in two rows all the way to the river, like at some of the plantations we passed."

Jacques laughed at her enthusiasm. "But, Madeleine, those rows of trees led to large houses. Our trees will lead to this little shack. Don't you think people will laugh at our being so ostentatious? I can hear them now: 'and here are the Boulignys of Magnolia Row Shack.'"

Madeleine felt confident, finally in control of her future. "It won't always be a shack, but the name should have 'magnolia' in it. How about 'Magnolia Grove'?"

"It sounds lovely, the perfect name for a big plantation.

But must I remind you again that I am not a planter. I am a soldier and a gentleman."

"*Oui*, Jacques. But we can use the land to plant a small garden, *n'est-ce pas*? And perhaps we can make the house livable in case we are not able to pay our rent."

Jacques' good mood was dampened at this reminder of his gambling loss and his inability to take care of his wife properly. He resented her for pointing it out. He was reminded again of the reason he was in New Orleans instead of Paris or some other established citadel of gracious living in the Old World—a reason he was careful not to reveal to Madeleine or his fellow officers. His family, embarrassed by his youthful irresponsibility and his gambling debts there, had strongly urged him to leave France. They had agreed to pay him a small but regular sum if he would accept a commission in the army and go to Canada. He had hoped to make a fresh new start on the frontier there, but his gambling habit traveled with him from Canada to Louisiana. He vowed once more to himself to moderate his gambling.

Trying hard to look more cheerful than he felt, Jacques followed Madeleine into the house, caught up again by her enthusiasm. The three-room wooden house with a roof made of fan-shaped palmetto branches was badly built and in need of repair. But Madeleine, remembering her parents' home, knew it was livable. There were cracks between the walls, and the shutters on the narrow windows were ready to fall off. The front door would not close all the way, and the back door was missing. How beautiful it will be, Madeleine thought, after I work on it.

The only furniture was a dirty corn-shuck mattress on the rough pine floor and a crudely built table with a backless bench. There was only an open fireplace for cooking. Madeleine got busy. She and Laff made brooms out of branches and swept the place as clean as possible. She had Lying Boy take the mattress outside to beat the dust out of it. As she worked, she made mental notes of what had to be done the next time they came.

Jacques, seldom around when Madeleine did housework at the Parraults', was amazed at her activity. "Madeleine, anyone would think you are a peasant girl the way you are acting."

This statement stopped Madeleine cold for a moment. Had she gone back full circle to the life she had wanted to escape, backbreaking work on a farm? It was true that she had wanted to get away from that, but this, she thought, is different. This is my land, or at least mine and Jacques's, not someone else's. I will work it and tame it and make my home upon it. She remembered what Captain Beauchamp had said about new beginnings in a new land. It made no sense to leave her old life behind unless she used it to make a better new one. And use it she would. She continued to clean without answering her husband.

That night Madeleine slept in her own home for the first time in her life. She lay beside her husband on the corn shuck mattress covered only by the blanket from the picnic basket. A fire was banked in the fireplace to take the chill off. They were alone in the house because the Indian couple preferred to sleep on pine straw outside rather than on the hard floor. Jacques stirred and moved closer to her. For once Madeleine did not stiffen and move away. They had made love earlier, and it had been different from other times. Jacques had seen a side of his wife that day he had never seen before. He felt that he was looking at and touching a different woman, a woman he did not totally approve of but one he could not take for granted. He felt he had seen some of what Madeleine had kept hidden from him.

For the first time, he treated his wife's body with more respect and used a gentler touch. For the first time Madeleine had felt more relaxed, thus softer and more yielding when he touched her intimately. She felt something comforting and pleasant as he moved rhythmically inside her. When he climaxed, she felt closer to him, not invaded as she usually did. Perhaps she could learn to like this after all, she thought. She looked out the open back door at the stars and felt hopeful.

Chapter 18

Madeleine stood up to rest her back after hours of picking butterbeans in the hot August sun. She wore a high-necked, long-sleeved dress, a large straw hat, and old cotton gloves to protect her skin from the sun. If she became freckled, she would never pass as a lady on her more and more infrequent visits to town, and Jacques would be furious. She would be revealed as the peasant she had been.

Her only concession to the heat was her bare feet. She tried to bury them underneath the top layer of dirt so they would not be scorched. She wiped her hands for the hundredth time that day. How she hated getting her hands dirty, she thought with irony; but a farmer cannot avoid dirty hands. And a farmer she had been for the past four months, not the gracious mistress of a plantation.

She had persuaded Jacques to allow her and the two Indians to move to Magnolia Grove, as she insisted on calling it, and live there through the summer and fall, at least until winter, so they could grow their own food. Jacques hated the idea; but, since he could no longer afford to pay rent at the Parraults' or feed them, he agreed. An added inducement was that he could live in the barracks whenever he was in New Orleans, which was most of the time, and live much like a single man again. He found it more difficult to be without Lying Boy than Madeleine, but she could not stay on the farm with only Laff as protection. Also, Lying Boy himself obviously wanted to stay at the farm with the two women.

After bidding the Parraults tearful goodbyes and promises to visit and move back when winter came, Madeleine had her small store of furniture, household goods, and her prized *casquette* moved from the attic to a flatboat and floated upriver to her own home, such as it was. She told an unobservant Jacques that Anne Parrault had given her most of the furniture from their room because she had no space for it in her house. She had even given them the feather mattress and iron bedstead, Madeleine lied. He chose to believe her explanation or he would be forced to think his wife was more enterprising than he was.

Madeleine, with the help of the two Indians and Jacques's infrequent and reluctant help, transformed the house as she had their room at the Parraults'. In short order, a back door was hung, shutters repaired, and the palmetto roof replaced with cypress shingles. Bright curtains were hung inside, and rag rugs laid on planed pine floors. Though Madeleine would have preferred the Indian couple to stay in the house with her in the small back room, Jacques would not hear of it and actually lent a hand building a small shed attached to the back of the house, but which technically could be said to be separate. When she discovered that Jacques could do simple carpentry, she persuaded him to add a gallery, or porch, to the front of the house and hang a swing made of cypress slabs and rope.

With the same relentless efficiency, she cleared fifteen acres of fertile bottomland near the swamp. She and the two Indians cut brush, dug up stumps, and burned off excess vegetation. Then she planted her vegetable garden, deliberately planning for a surplus that would have to be sold to avoid waste. She visited her blonde, blue-eyed German friends, Klaus and Hannah Mueller, at the nearby German settlement and got advice on which vegetables flourished in the hot humid Louisiana climate. She struck a bargain with them. In exchange for her teaching them and their three small boys to read, write, and properly speak French a few hours a week, Klaus lent her a mule and sometimes helped her with the plowing. The Muellers also brought her the few needed supplies she could afford from New Orleans when they took their produce to market every weekend. Madeleine thought enviously that, with the ever-pregnant Hannah, she would be able to exchange her services for years to come.

To her delight, she discovered several pecan, peach, and mulberry trees growing near the house, greatly supplementing their meager food supply of mostly squirrels, rabbits, and deer killed by Lying Boy and catfish and perch caught by Laff in the river. Klaus also pointed out that the strange-looking plants growing wild along the river were indigo plants, a frequent oddity along the Mississippi. He showed her how to consolidate and expand the size of the indigo growing in random patches and to be sold later for dye.

She had thought she might be lonely, especially at night with only Lying Boy and Laff and her books for company, but she found that she was too tired to do anything but fall into bed at night and sleep. She hated the endless, backbreaking work. Sometimes she felt despair over having chosen a life so similar to the one she had escaped when she went to work for the de Mandevilles, but she kept doggedly working and pushing Lying Boy and Laff. She knew the difference was that this was her land, hers and Jacques's. This was her only chance to prosper and live a life with any dignity. Realizing this, she felt exhilarated that she might use her skills and intelligence to make their future better.

During the remainder of summer, after the planting was done and she had a little more time, she was able to do some work that she enjoyed. She painstakingly transplanted young magnolia trees to form two parallel rows leading from the house to the river. She hoped that, by the time they were big enough to be noticed from boats on the river, she would have a house worthy of them. She also planted roses and crepe myrtle around the house to add color and fragrance. To Jacques's amusement and the Muellers' wonder, she planted an elaborate flower and hedge garden, a miniature version of the one at the de Mandeville estate. She asked the Muellers to bring her some cuttings of the recently imported fig and orange trees, which seemed to flourish in this climate, and planted them.

Each time Jacques came for a visit he was amazed at the changes in the place. He had thought a genteel, well-bred girl like Madeleine would soon tire of her hobby when she saw how hard life was in what he considered to be the wilderness. When she did not give up, he was puzzled and began to wonder if she had told him the entire truth about her background. She was obviously familiar with the customs and manners of the ruling class, but where did she learn how to perform the menial tasks he now saw her doing?

Madeleine tried to act the lady overseeing her servants' work as much as possible when Jacques was around, but he was no fool. He saw the calluses on her hands, and even he could tell that it took more than two Indians to accomplish what had been done there. "How the hell did you learn how to do hard farm work?"

She minimized what she had done. "Oh, Lying Boy and Klaus did most of it." Since he had no idea how to handle the situation if she were lying, he simply pushed the problem to the back of his mind and enjoyed his freedom from responsibility. Fortunately, perhaps for them both, he never stayed long. He missed the gaiety of New Orleans and soon made excuses to return, pleading military duties.

Then it was time to harvest her large garden. As Madeleine had planned, she had much more food than her small family could eat, even after some of it could be dried and preserved for use during the winter. So she sent Lying Boy downriver to New Orleans with the Muellers every Saturday night to sell their surplus vegetables and even some pecans and peaches. She knew she would get better prices if she went herself, but she had to protect Jacques' reputation as a provider. She knew she would be allowed to continue only if his pride were not injured.

Even with Lying Boy selling their produce—with the Mueller's help—she made a nice profit. She was able to pay for the seeds she had bought on credit, buy a few more household goods, and have enough left over to plant rice next spring in the frequently flooded cypress swamps on their land. She hid the extra money in the lining of her *casquette*, for she knew it would never do for Jacques to discover it. Besides hurting his pride by her succeeding where he had failed, he would surely take it for his gambling. The only way to keep his gambling within bounds, she believed, was to appear to remain poor.

Chapter 19

By November Madeleine, Lying Boy, Laff, the feather bed, and the *casquette* were back in New Orleans with the Parraults. Jacques had insisted that it would be dangerous to stay on their land relatively unprotected in view of the increasing Indian trouble. In the months Madeleine had been away, the town seemed to have grown enormously. She found it a relief in many ways to be back in what passed for civilization. The domestic duties she helped Anne with seemed like child's play after her hard work on the farm, but she missed being in her own home. Whatever she was doing, her head was full of improvements she wanted to make on the house and the land. She planned how much rice she should plant and where. She wondered if she dared to buy a slave and plant tobacco.

She found it hard to resume her social activities after her long months of solitude. Suzanne invited the other *casquette* girls, at least those still living in New Orleans, and their families and Sister Pauline to a tea given in her good friend Madeleine's honor. Madeleine found it a particularly trying occasion. Suzanne made too many jokes about Madeleine becoming a farmer.

"I don't know what possessed you to spend the whole summer in the wilderness with only two Indians for company. Are you sure you are French? You must be one of those awful British Protestants—or even worse, a Quaker— interested only in work and religion, never in having fun. I hear you worked like a peasant."

Madeleine caught Jacques averting his gaze, as if he were embarrassed by Suzanne's words.

Another problem that depressed Madeleine was the fact that most of the *casquette* girls, including Suzanne, were new mothers. They all took pride in showing her their babies. When, they all wanted to know, was Madeleine going to start her family? Suzanne showed off a sturdy-looking little boy named Yves. She looked riper and more voluptuous than ever. Madeleine noticed that Jacques's eyes followed the blonde beauty. She wondered if he thought he had married the wrong woman.

Even Sister Pauline asked her if she were pregnant. "*Ma petite*, you will make such a wonderful mother. You must pray that God blesses you with children. Perhaps you have been working too hard. If you become too muscular, you might not be able to conceive."

Madeleine could not bear to talk about her inadequacies any longer, so she changed the subject. "Has *les Belles Soeurs* returned to New Orleans? I wonder if it might have brought any new settlers."

Sister Pauline thought her question odd. "Ships are bringing settlers all the time. It is rare to walk down Royal

Street without hearing three or four different languages. But, *oui, les Belles Soeurs* did return many times. I often see Captain Beauchamp. He has made this route a full-time occupation, though he brings mostly supplies, not passengers."

Madeleine held her breath hoping she would say more. As if reading her mind, Sister Pauline said rather shyly, "He asked about you. That was right after you moved to your farm, I believe. He seemed surprised that you had married, though I can't think why he should be. After all, you had little choice but to marry. He said he was planning to buy a home in New Orleans so he could stop over longer between voyages."

Madeleine's head was spinning. Could he have changed his mind about marrying? She remembered how terrible a life it had seemed to her if she married him, always alone and waiting for a husband to return from the sea. She thought ironically of how little time Jacques was with her. He might as well be at sea.

She soon asked Jacques to take her home, in spite of his protests that she was too solemn to be truly French.

Chapter 20

With Madeleine safely settled in New Orleans, Jacques felt free to go on a mission to Fort Rosalie for Governor Perier. It was generally known, even by the Indians, that the Company wanted the Indians to be forced to leave the colony. The fact that the Indians knew about this policy and might retaliate in some way worried Perier. His other worry was Etcheparre, his own choice to command Fort Rosalie, which was stuck in the midst of Natchez country. He had continued to get reports of Etcheparre's unwise handling of the Indians. He had heard that Etcheparre planned to take over the major Natchez village there and force the Indians out. His advisors believed that the Natchez would not merely surrender to this plan. Perier hated to admit he had made a mistake by appointing and then reappointing Etcheparre, so he sent Jacques to make an informal investigation, hoping to be reassured. Madeleine sent him off with pleas to visit her friend Delphine, who had moved to Fort Rosalie with the Kaintuck she had married, but she had little hope he would do it.

When Jacques arrived at Fort Rosalie, he found Etcheparre and several of his officers preparing to go to the Natchez village, White Apple, about six miles from the French settlement, for a celebration in Etcheparre's honor. Jacques was told that the Natchez were surrendering their village the next day. Etcheparre, a short, stocky, big-bellied man, could not hide his smugness or his greed at his coup. He invited Jacques to join the celebration, thinking Jacques was merely passing through.

The French officers were welcomed royally at the beautiful Natchez village. Jacques could see why Etcheparre wanted the village so badly. The carefully cultivated apple crops alone would make him a rich man. The young chief of the village, Great Sun, greeted them with a long eloquent speech. The French were fed a lavish feast of wild pig, plied again and again with liquor, and given willing Indian maidens to amuse them. Jacques was careful not to eat or drink too much. He noticed that Etcheparre was indulging himself totally.

During the feast, after Etcheparre's tongue had been loosened by drink, Jacques managed to question him about his acquisition of the village. He was amazed at the man's blind arrogance.

"Of course there was no problem in getting them to agree. What could they do? They are no match for us. I was generous with them: I did not turn them out immediately."

"What do you mean?"

"They asked for a couple of months' time find a place to go and to make preparations, and I gave it to them."

Etcheparre leaned over cozily to Jacques and whispered, "Just between you and me, they offered to pay me a barrel of corn, some furs, fowls, and bear's oil per cabin for the privilege of staying longer. And there are eighty cabins in the village," he proclaimed with satisfaction.

"Aren't you afraid the postponement might be a trick? It's hard to believe they would just give up their home for generations without a fight."

Etcheparre gave him an angry look and said in a surly tone, "Whom have you been talking to? My lieutenant, Mace?"

Jacques tried to dispel his suspicions. "*Non*, I came to you as soon as I arrived at Fort Rosalie. What did Lieutenant Mace tell you? Here, have some more brandy."

Etcheparre took the brandy and belched. "Mace is a coward. So are the others. I threw them in the stockade."

"Oh? I bet that taught them a lesson. What did they say to you?" he repeated.

Etcheparre answered reluctantly, "They said a plan was afoot to attack all the French settlements. Mace claimed there would be a massacre. I threw the cowards in the stockade," he repeated drunkenly.

Jacques tried to reason with him logically, "Are you aware that d'Artaguette's dispatch, written only last year, estimated that the Indian settlements on the banks of principal rivers in Louisiana could produce 17,000 warriors?"

Etcheparre's eyes glazed over with boredom. "That is only if all the Indian nations got together. They will never do that. They fight among themselves too much."

Jacques tried to hide his uneasiness. He was more determined than ever to stay sober and watchful. He sat for hours, sipping his drink slowly, and watched the drunken revelry. A young Indian woman sat down beside him and offered him more to drink. He was pleased to see that she was slim and beautiful with a well-rounded body, soft and inviting. When he asked her what her name was, she said it was Lame Doe. She took his hand and led him to a cabin. He noticed that she limped slightly, but it seemed to be her only imperfection, aside from being an Indian. In spite of his worry about his mission, he began to get excited.

When they entered the darkened cabin, he could hardly wait to remove her soft deerskin dress and touch her smooth brown body. As his eyes adjusted to the dim light, he was startled by the sight of an old white-haired Indian squaw sitting by the fireplace.

"This is Brar Pique, or Pricked Arm, the old princess, mother to the Great Sun and to me. She wishes to talk to you. If you like, I will come back later." Lame Doe smiled shyly and left him alone with Pricked Arm.

Jacques hid his disappointment and said courteously, "You wished to speak with me?"

"Yes, I want to warn you of my people's plan to attack Fort Rosalie very soon," she said simply.

Jacques sat down in shock. "*Mon Dieu*, is this true? If it is, why would you tell me?"

"I do not want your people hurt. I have lived among them for many moons. It is said that my son, the Great Sun, has for his father a French officer. I do not know if this is true, but it makes my son more careful to show our people he is not partial to the French."

Jacques was still suspicious. "I cannot believe you would betray your own people. What would you gain from this?"

"I do not wish my people to be hurt. Each year more

pale-faced warriors come across the water to our land. They have knowledge of things we do not. If my son's plan succeeds, the Natchez will be tracked down and killed. I do not want this to happen."

"But if I convince Etcheparre of this plan, surely you know that he will arm the fort. Then most of the village, including you and your son, will be killed during the attack." Jacques still did not understand her motives.

"If my son and his warriors see that you are strengthening your fortifications, they will not attack. They are not fools."

Jacques saw her point but was still skeptical. "This may be true, but didn't he expect Governor Perier to send out troops to punish your village?"

She hesitated before she answered, "I did not want to tell you this, but our council met in secret to plan an alliance of the Yazoos, the Chickasaws, and the Choctaws. They sent out messengers to ask them to attack every French settlement in the colony on the same day."

Jacques could not hide his amazement. "This is hard to believe. The Choctaws too? What was the response?"

"My son said they all agreed. Each tribe was given a bundle of sticks. They were to take out a stick each day. When only one stick was left, they were to attack."

"Quite ingenuous," Jacques replied. "And all the French would be wiped out. There would be no one to punish the Natchez."

"I slipped in the temple where the sticks were kept and added a few sticks to put off the time of attack, but I know there cannot be many left."

Jacques was still puzzled. "I am grateful to you for this information. Why did your son tell you about the plan? He must have known you were sympathetic to the French."

Pricked Arm answered patiently, "I tricked my son into telling me, using my age, my position as his mother, and promises of wise counsel. I had already guessed much of their plan because of the secret meetings. The men swore not to tell the women because so many of us are close to French soldiers."

Jacques had one last question. "Why do you tell me of this plan? Why not tell Etcheparre or one of his officers?"

"Etcheparre is a stupid pig. He would not believe an old Indian woman. I did tell several of his officers. First I hinted at part of it. When no action was taken, I told Mace, his lieutenant, outright. Etcheparre did not believe any of them."

Jacques agreed with her on that. "*Oui*, he told me himself that he had them thrown in the stockade."

Pricked Arm continued, "I tell you because I know of no one else to tell. It is said you are sent by Perier. I know Etcheparre listens to you. I watched the two of you talking during the feast. Lame Doe told me you were trying to counsel him."

Jacques replied ruefully, "I am afraid he paid little heed to my words also. In any case, he is too drunk tonight to listen to anyone. I will try my luck tomorrow when he is sober. If I don't get anywhere, I promise you I will appeal to Perier."

"Do not wait too long. I believe the attack is soon. I can tell by the way the men are acting," cautioned the old woman. "Now shall I call Lame Doe back to amuse you? She is my daughter, and I have trained her to be pleasing."

"*Non, merci beaucoup*. I think it best that I am not distracted during my stay here. I will return to the fort now.

If you find out anything else, send a message to the house of *La Loire des Orsins*, where I will spend the night." He bowed to the woman and backed out of the cabin.

The next morning, November 29, was a beautiful, crisp fall day. Jacques got up early and sent a message to Etcheparre saying that he wanted to see him. When the messenger returned saying that Etcheparre did not want to be disturbed until nine o'clock, Jacques determined to wait until he saw the commander, then leave for New Orleans. He sat down with seven other officers staying in the barracks-like house to eat a leisurely breakfast.

While the unsuspecting French were starting the morning with their customary routine and most of the officers were nursing hangovers, the Natchez were busy executing their plan for an attack that day. For miles around Fort Rosalie, small groups of Natchez Indians were knocking on French settlers' doors and asking to borrow some powder or shot for hunting.

At the same time a large procession of Natchez warriors arrived at the fort, bearing the gifts they had promised Etcheparre for letting them stay the extra time in their village. A bleary-eyed Etcheparre was delighted to see them and welcomed them warmly. He was greatly relieved at this show of cooperation and friendliness. He ordered the officers in the stockade to be released so they could see how wrong they were to predict a massacre.

As these Indians scattered and placed themselves throughout the fort, another group of warriors crept down the hill to the bank of the river where a large galley was anchored at the dock. They simultaneously fired at the men on the ship. This was the signal to begin the massacre. The Indians inside the fort and at French settlers' homes outside the fort heard the gunfire and began firing so quickly themselves that it sounded like one huge explosion.

Neither the settlers nor the soldiers nor their families had a chance. They were totally unprepared. While Etcheparre sat in his parlor smoking the peace pipe and watching Indian dancers, approximately three hundred settlers were clubbed to death or shot, many of them with their own weapons. This task took less than half an hour. Etcheparre ran into his garden to hide when he heard the shooting and screaming. The Indians considered him so beneath their contempt that he was not given the dignity of being shot by a warrior. His death was saved until the last; then the lowest, dirtiest Indian in the village was given the job of clubbing him to death in his garden.

Fewer than twenty people escaped Fort Rosalie. One of these was Jacques. When he and the other officers in *des Orsins'* house heard the shooting and looked out the window, they were horrified at the grisly sight. The Indians were cutting off the heads of the soldiers, some not yet dead, and tossing them in a pile. Children and women who were not pregnant were being spared, but they were forced to watch as the Indians danced and caroused around the pyramids of heads. Even more horrifying to Jacques was the fate of the women who were pregnant. Their bellies were slashed open and their fetuses ripped out and thrown to the ground as they watched. Jacques knew he would never forget the agonized looks on their faces.

By some stroke of luck, *des Orsins'* house was one of the last attacked in the fort. The officers were able to prepare themselves. They persuaded Jacques and one other officer to make a run for New Orleans and warn Perier. While they covered the two men's exit with gunfire out the front, Jacques and the other officer barely escaped out the back. The six officers left managed to hold the Indians off all day and killed eight of them. La Loire des Orsins was caught on horseback not far from his house and killed four Indians before he was killed himself. The attack cost the Indians only twelve men. One hundred and fifty French soldiers were killed.

Jacques learned later that two men were spared. One was Mayeux, a wagoner who was used to transport French goods to the public square. The other was Lebeau, a tailor. His task was to alter the clothes of the French to fit the Indians. The three hundred women and children whose lives were spared were taken as slaves. Finally, they set fire to the French people's houses.

When Jacques returned home that night after reporting to Perier, he could not stop shaking. He lay in bed wide-awake all night and allowed Madeleine to hold him and comfort him.

Though there were attacks later at the Yazoos, St. Claude, and Natchitoches, New Orleans had been forewarned. On the first of December, six hundred Choctaw warriors arrived at the mouth of the Chefuncte River at Lake Pontchartrain asking for permission to present Governor Perier with the calumet of peace. Perier wisely offered to receive only the chief and thirty warriors. Realizing the French were suspicious of them, the Choctaws returned to their villages, killing and stealing some cattle along the way.

Chapter 21

Two months after the Natchez massacre at Fort Rosalie, the three hundred women, children, and Negro slaves taken prisoner still had not been returned or rescued. Madeleine and her friends prayed for them daily. Jacques and every other able-bodied man in the colony were kept busy defending French settlements and boats that brought supplies up the Mississippi.

Hostilities continued between the Natchez and the French. Though the widespread, organized attacks on the French did not materialize as the Natchez had planned, there were successful attacks on French settlements at the Yazoos and St. Claude. New Orleans was horrified to learn that, before the attack on St. Claude, a woman used as hostage during negotiations was burned by the Natchez in front of the French settlement.

At least the Choctaws were back in the fold. When they learned that the Natchez were not willing to share their booty of battle with them, the Choctaws made peace with the French. With their superior numbers, they helped the French drive out the Natchez and recover most of the prisoners. Jacques was a part of that battle and survived without any physical wounds, but afterwards he found that he had trouble falling asleep at night without drinking himself numb.

For weeks he would not discuss the battle with Madeleine; then finally one night he told her of an incident that still gave him nightmares. "Madeleine, they are devils, these Natchez. At first we asked the vermin to surrender, sending Du Parc with a flag of peace. They shot at him and scared him so badly he dropped the flag. When the Indians opened the gates for a moment to pick it up, some of our own imprisoned women prisoners slipped out the gate and ran to our camp. The bastards then took some of the children and impaled them on the stakes of the fort."

Madeleine shuddered and took his shaking hands. "Ah *non, non,* they could not have."

Jacques continued angrily. "Of course they did. It was nothing to them. We had to watch helplessly as those children died. I cannot forget their screams. For once I was glad we had no children."

Madeleine's heart softened toward him and she held him and stroked his hair. He immediately tensed, pulled away, and continued, almost as if he were talking to himself, "I will admit they are cunning devils. When they finally realized they were outnumbered and surrendered the captives, they escaped with all their stolen goods."

Madeleine was puzzled. "How could they escape if they were outnumbered?"

Jacques answered her irritably, "While we were

celebrating the return of the prisoners and getting ready to attack them the next day, the traitorous dogs sneaked out during the night, taking everything with them except a few old rags."

"I still do not understand. You say you were getting ready to attack them. Wouldn't that have been dishonest after they surrendered and returned the prisoners?"

Jacques became indignant, "Do you think we should have let them go unpunished after what they did? Haven't you heard anything I said? How long do you think it would be before they attacked again?"

Madeleine decided to yield that point and try to discuss strategy with him to keep him talking to her. "In that case, why did you wait so long to attack? Why not immediately after they surrendered?"

Jacques lashed out at her angrily. "What the hell do you know of battles? Do you think because you can run a picayune farm you can handle any kind of men's affairs?"

Madeleine recoiled at first from his words and then reached out her hand to him, trying once more to soothe him. "*Non, mon cher*, you are right. I know nothing of these matters."

Jacques pulled away again. "Don't try to coddle me; I don't need it. We will chase down those murdering Indians and kill every one of them. Then I will be able to sleep again."

Madeleine resumed her distant manner then and reproved him. "*Mais*, Jacques, they have innocent women and children also. They must not be made to suffer."

"May they all rot in hell. They're vicious animals, every one of them."

"And Lying Boy and Laff, are they animals too?"

Jacques would not relent. "*Oui,* they happen to be domesticated animals. The Choctaws would have murdered us in our beds if I had not warned Perier of the Natchez attack so that we would appear prepared. They change their loyalties with the wind. Look how fast Lying Boy switched his allegiance from me to you."

"Jacques, I did not know you minded that Lying Boy stayed with me on the farm."

"I don't mind. You needed him there. It was his eagerness to be there that I minded."

Madeleine got a glimpse of his loneliness, but did not know how to comfort him. His pride would not allow him to show that he needed her. He opened another bottle and kept drinking. Madeleine felt sadder and wished she were back at Magnolia Grove.

As the rescued prisoners from the Natchez massacre straggled wearily into New Orleans, the city welcomed them with compassion. Those few who were healthy were taken into people's homes and fed and clothed. The sick were taken to Charity Hospital and cared for tenderly by the Ursuline nuns. Jacques protested when Madeleine tirelessly helped the nuns at the hospital, but she defied him because of how badly she was needed.

The rescued slaves were cared for in a separate room from the whites. Madeleine was the only white woman besides the nuns willing to help nurse the Negroes. Two of her favorites were Moses and his woman, Rima. Moses was a short, wiry, good-natured man in his thirties who had been sold downriver from the Carolinas. Rima, a young, strong woman not long out of the jungle, towered above him. She had a reputation among the Fort Rosalie people as a troublemaker, but Moses's loving eyes seldom left his half-tamed mate.

Though Rima was in perfect health, Moses suffered from a gunshot wound that had become infected. The doctor wanted to remove the arm immediately when Moses was brought in. Madeleine, seeing the fear in Moses' and Rima's eyes at the sight of the knife, talked the doctor into waiting until morning so she could have a chance at getting the infection down.

She and Rima worked all night, cleaning his wound and sponging off the vile-smelling pus. They took turns putting cold compresses on his head to get his fever down. By the next morning his arm passed inspection with the doctor. Moses and Rima grinned their gratitude at Madeleine, for they both knew Moses would have been of little use with only one arm.

Moses and Rima had been left without masters, as had been many of the slaves, so Madeleine decided to sacrifice some of her small store of money to buy them. Sister Pauline carried her request to Governor Perier himself; and, because of Madeleine's unselfish volunteer work in the hospital and the school, Perier awarded her the slaves as a gift. Sister Pauline did not pass on the information that he thought they would not fetch a good price anyway because of Moses's stiff arm and Rima's wildness. Nor did she tell Madeleine that Governor Perier mentioned Jacques's drinking and gambling, hinting that the couple could not afford to buy the Negroes at any price. Madeleine was relieved she did not have to pay for them. The longer she could prevent Jacques from knowing about her money, the longer she would be able to prevent his losing it in a faro game.

Madeleine contributed Rima's and Moses's services to the Ursuline nuns until spring planting. Her generosity served two purposes: the nuns received some badly needed help, and the Negro couple had a place to stay for the winter, since there was no room for them at the Parraults'. Madeleine got another benefit she did not expect. Her undesirable slaves became very desirable indeed. Moses's arm healed much better than expected thanks to Madeleine's nursing and the extra food she smuggled in to Moses and Rima, plus Rima's constant massages. And to everyone's surprise, Rima converted to Christianity; that and her devotion to Madeleine calmed her down considerably.

Sister Pauline was a little suspicious of Rima's conversion and told Madeleine that she thought it was to please her new mistress. Rima obviously admired Madeleine and tried to imitate her quiet dignity, no small feat for the volatile Negro. Madeleine shared Sister Pauline's doubts when she surprised Rima with her head bowed piously fingering her rosaries to the beat of an African chant. On closer inspection, Madeleine found long coarse black hairs intertwined with rosary beads. They looked suspiciously like Indian hairs. She decided to let Rima worship as she pleased.

Chapter 22

New Orleans continued to be unsettled and fearful of attack throughout that year of 1730. Governor Perier took measures to protect the colony, for there was still trouble with stray Natchez and, as always, the Chickasaws. He established eight small forts between Natchez and New Orleans so the settlers in the surrounding areas would have a refuge. When some Swiss mercenaries arrived, he made them a part of his troops. Then he forced all the Indians between La Balize and Natchez to move, except for the Tunicas, who had always been friends of the French.

The people of New Orleans had not only the Indians to fear but also the Negro slaves. A few Chickasaws had incited some Negroes to revolt against their French masters and butcher them in their beds. Fortunately, they were found out in time. To make an example of them and to discourage future rebellions, eight men were tied to a wagon wheel and tortured by breaking their bones. One woman was hanged.

When Jacques matter-of-factly told Madeleine about these atrocities, committed by Indians, Negroes, and Frenchmen, she had trouble taking it in. They seemed like stories told about another people in another land. Was this place so primitive then? She worried about what was happening to Jacques. He seemed more and more callous and distant. His old spontaneous passion, which had originally fascinated the cool Madeleine, came to the surface less and less. It was as if he had to protect himself from feeling anything. As a result, they grew even further apart.

When Jacques was in New Orleans, he spent little time with Madeleine. He even stopped objecting to her working at Charity Hospital, so she continued to help the nuns there after the Fort Rosalie captives left. They seldom made love now, a change that gave Madeleine mixed feelings. When Jacques did make an overture, he was usually drunk. She began to associate sex with the smell of liquor, an association that did nothing to make her more receptive. She knew he spent a lot of time at O'Brien's Pub, owned by Marie, Jacques's old mistress, and Michael O'Brien. Evidently their bar was doing very well.

Robert Parrault, forgetting Jacques's old association with Marie, described it to Madeleine and Anne. He laughed and said, "It is strange to see so many Frenchmen frequent this typically Irish pub. They drink Irish whiskey and Irish coffee instead of sipping wine or cognac. Every night Marie brings in a big batch of cabbage and potato stew, and Michael teaches the customers Irish ditties. You should hear them sung in a French accent."

Madeleine pretended to have only a casual interest. "Why would Frenchmen go there instead of their own bars? Wouldn't they be more comfortable patronizing their countrymen's bars?'

"I think we go there because it's different. It is the only one of its kind. Also, the British colonists don't like to go there because it is what they are used to upriver. For some reason they like the French bars, where they get cheated and robbed."

One day she ran into Marie at the market. The red-haired woman seemed to be making an attempt to look more respectable now that she was married. She wore a plain, loose, brown dress over her very pregnant body. She wore no paint on her face; only her hair with that outrageous carrot red attracted attention. The two women pretended that they did not know each other. Madeleine knew they were both thinking about that day when the *casquette* girls arrived and Marie spat on Madeleine's skirt. She had to stifle a sudden urge to spit on Marie's swollen belly. Thinking of how shocked the other ladies, not to mention Marie, would be if the always composed Madeleine Bouligny suddenly acted like an alley cat, Madeleine's mouth turned up at the corners in a quick, tight smile and her eyes glinted with mischief. Marie caught the expression on her face and almost smiled back, thinking Madeleine was making a friendly overture. Then the expression on Madeleine's face passed and the moment was gone.

Madeleine knew she really had nothing to fear from Marie, who had been a common trollop. Jacques was too conscious of his social status to have any real interest in her. She was not so secure when she saw him around Suzanne, however. Jacques frequently forced Madeleine to attend parties with him at the Chauvins', and she watched with controlled fury as he basked in Suzanne's obvious attentions.

Suzanne had become the most sought-after hostess in New Orleans. She was beautiful, animated, and rich. She could afford to entertain lavishly. Had her parties not been a success, they would still have been widely attended because most of the town owed her husband money. She had quickly become bored with the middle-aged Jean Claude and now amused herself by flirting with younger handsomer men. Jacques had a special appeal for her because he was Madeleine's husband. As long as Suzanne kept her flirting within bounds, her reputation remained safe. She had the added protection of being a married matron with a child, plus being one of the spotless *casquette* girls.

Madeleine felt drab and inadequate in the same room with this lovely, gilded butterfly flitting from guest to guest. She simply did not have the knack for light chatter and felt foolish flirting even with her own husband. Rather than appear foolish, she preferred to retain her dignity, at the risk of seeming staid. More than once she was asked by strangers if she were really British instead of French.

At one dinner party given by the Chauvins, Suzanne seated herself by Jacques and poured him glass after glass of wine. He had ignored Madeleine the whole evening. Suzanne was resplendent in a pink satin dress, daringly low cut. She leaned into Jacques at every opportunity and laughed gaily at his every witticism. Madeleine sat quietly in her old white wool, now beginning to look worn, and tried not to notice them. She wondered if she should spend some of her seed money for rice on a new dress instead but knew that would not make her into the warm, fun-loving kind of wife Jacques would like.

After dinner Suzanne insisted on taking Madeleine

into the nursery to show off her little boy. Yves, her golden-haired baby, looked so innocent and sweet in his sleep that Madeleine could hardly believe he was Suzanne's.

"He is a lovely child, Suzanne; you are right to be proud of him."

"He is truly my life," responded Suzanne primly.

"I can see that," said Madeleine, thinking that Suzanne was playing the Madonna role to the hilt.

"You must have one of your own soon, my dear. You would be so much more fulfilled. Everybody says so."

"Does everybody? And what make you think I am not fulfilled now?" Madeleine began to get impatient.

"Ah, Madeleine, you can speak frankly with me. We are old friends. Anyone can see you and Jacques are not well suited. Jacques is so alive and passionate, and you are so...."

"So?" Madeleine encouraged with icy politeness.

Suzanne pretended to search for just the right word. "Reserved. Yes, so reserved and ladylike always. If you had children, it would make you a whole woman."

Madeleine was blinded by fury. She grabbed Suzanne by the top of her pink satin dress, her knuckles digging into those soft breasts, and hissed in a low voice. "Perhaps you would like for Jacques and everyone else to know how much of a whole woman *you* really are. How fertile you really are. They would all be so impressed if I told them you had had not one, but *two* children."

Suzanne paled. "You wouldn't dare! Nobody would believe you."

"Wouldn't they? One advantage to being pious and sober and perfectly respectable is that nobody doubts your word."

Suzanne began to believe her and pleaded, "Please, Madeleine, do not tell anyone. It would ruin me. My life is going so well. I didn't mean to offend you. You are my trusted friend."

Madeleine released her dress and grabbed her arm with work-hardened fingers. "Then be *my* trusted friend and never ever again ask me when I plan to have children." She squeezed the arm with all her strength. "And stay away from my husband. Do not get within breathing distance of him. Do you understand?"

Suzanne looked at her with new respect. "*Oui*, whatever you say. I did not mean to intrude." When Madeleine released her arm, she gasped with relief.

"*Bien*," said Madeleine evenly. "Now perhaps you would like to return to your guests."

When Suzanne left the room, Madeleine began to shake, first with anger and then with silent laughter. Too much of a lady, am I? Well, I surprised us both. My quick-to-anger old papa would have been proud of me. I sounded just like him.

Chapter 23

Madeleine's second spring in Louisiana finally arrived, and she eagerly prepared to return to Magnolia Grove. This time it took two flatboats to take her, Lying Boy and Laff, Moses and Rima, plus enough lumber to build an additional room and a new cabin, bricks for covering the outside of the small main house, some new furniture, food and supplies, and sacks of her important seeds. She carried her precious rice seed in her *casquette*. She was uneasy that she had so little money left in it, but she was optimistic that by fall its lining, still her secret hiding place, would be bulging.

She carefully planned her departure for when she thought Jacques would not be in New Orleans so he would not see how many possessions she had accumulated. She was terrified that he would realize she had hidden money from him. She had given him the impression that the farm had merely broken even, supplying them and the Parraults with food for the year. Because she had spent no money on clothes, it had been easy to fool him. It would never occur to him that a woman, even Madeleine, would have money and not spend it on her appearance.

Madeleine had hugged and kissed the Parraults for the last time and climbed aboard. She and her servants were in high spirits. Lying Boy and Laff were delighted to leave the crowded town and return to the farm. Moses and Rima were anxious to see their new home, but a little nervous around the two Indians. Madeleine had explained that they were not like the Natchez, but the two Negroes were not convinced.

Just as they were ready to leave the dock, Jacques came running up and leaped aboard. Madeleine tried to hide her uneasiness and act glad to see him. He did not seem to notice her mood and, to her tremendous relief, did not seem to connect all the goods on the second flatboat with her. "Madeleine, I am so glad I caught you. I am afraid I have bad news for you. You may not want to go to the farm after all."

Madeleine's heart sank. "Why not? Have you lost it in a card game?" In her fear she forgot to be tactful.

Jacques replied in cold anger. "*Non*, I did not lose it. Have you no trust in me at all? Do you think I would gamble away *your* only home?"

Madeleine began to breathe easier and said a little guiltily, "Jacques, of course I trust you. I was so frightened I said the most awful thing I could think of. What is the bad news then?"

Jacques was only partly mollified by her apology and blurted out tactlessly, "It has nothing to do with my gambling, but we may lose most of the farm anyway."

"How?" Madeleine asked fearfully.

"Governor Perier told me that the Company is enforcing the ordinance that all land grants must be put under cultivation. Any land that is not will be reduced to twenty acres." He told her this with a note of satisfaction.

"Oh, no!" cried Madeleine. She sat down heavily on a box.

"How much will you have under cultivation this season? "

Madeleine answered dispiritedly, "I might be able to stretch it to twenty acres if I spread the plants farther apart to take up more acreage. I was going to plant a few acres of rice as an experiment. If they leave us with only twenty, plus the twenty under cultivation, we will never be able to expand. Magnolia Grove will always be nothing but a small farm. It will never be a plantation that people will look at from the river and admire."

Jacques said in surprise, "But it was never intended to be more than a farm to grow a few vegetables on. I always intended to sell most of the land." When Madeleine looked away and did not reply, Jacques began to get a glimpse of his wife's dreams. He felt like less than a man because he could not help her make them come true. Perhaps it would be better to lose the land right away than for her to spend years wishing for the impossible.

Jacques said gently, "*Ma cherie*, I am sorry that we will lose the land, but maybe it is for the best. You will not work so hard then. In any case, we have a year before they take it. Don't worry. I will take better care of you."

Madeleine did not answer. Giving up, he jumped off the flatboat without another word and walked in the direction of O'Brien's Pub. Madeleine stood on the flatboat as it floated away from the dock. She had never felt more alone, but as usual she kept her head and back erect and did not look back.

After a month on the farm, Madeleine almost wished for her easy life in New Orleans again. Already the weather was unbearably hot, and summer was only beginning. She and her four servants worked from dawn to many times after dark planting and making improvements. Moses turned out to be a skilled carpenter and bricklayer, so the house now had a sturdy brick exterior, giving it better insulation and a handsomer look. He and Rima lived in their own newly-built, small cabin in the back. They had adjusted quickly to the farm and proved to be tireless workers, devoted to Madeleine. Rima also turned out to be an excellent cook, specializing in hominy, which she cooked all day in the yard in a huge black iron pot that doubled as a wash-pot for clothes, gumbo (a fish-based stew loaded with roots and vegetables), and jambalaya (sometimes cooked with corn, sometimes with rice). This skill made her acceptable to the two Indians.

Lying Boy and Laff remained in the lean-to, satisfied with their lot in life. They were less reliable than the Negroes but, if pressed, would work. Lying Boy's biggest contribution was providing game for the table, and Laff's was fish. She had a knack for catching catfish and perch when no one else could; she had the patience to sit for hours to wait for a bite. They all ate well and lived in moderate comfort, but the threat of losing most of the land hung over Madeleine's head constantly. She kept working harder and pushing the servants to plant more and more. Once a week Lying Boy took her in a pirogue he had made to the

Muellers, where she resumed teaching their children in return for the use of their mule. Again, Klaus helped when he could.

When it came time to plant the rice, Madeleine pushed even harder. She was determined to plant as much as possible even if she could not harvest it all. She spent the last bit of money in her *casquette* for more rice seed to plant. Klaus and some of his friends, all sympathetic to her plight and valuing land themselves, helped out a few days. They managed to plant twenty acres of rice in her cypress swamp where the land could be naturally irrigated by flooding from the river's tide. Madeleine fell into bed exhausted every night. Some nights Rima would massage her neck with her strong fingers to help her sleep. Moses and Rima, both sensitive to her fear of losing such a large part of her land, became more like friends than slaves.

As summer set in, Laff and Rima had to slow down a little in their work, for both were pregnant. This seemed to create a bond between them finally, though with a competitive edge. They jabbered together in their broken French, and Moses and Lying Boy seemed to have a strut to their walks in spite of their exhaustion from work. One day Madeleine caught Laff and Rima comparing bellies, and she became even more depressed. It seemed that everything on this fertile land was breeding except her. Hannah Mueller also was *enceinte* again. Even the wild pig Lying Boy caught in the woods and put in a pen was breeding. Madeleine despaired of ever having a child. She also wondered if forty acres, left after the Company redeemed the uncultivated land, would support the growing number of people for whom she was responsible. It was ironic that she would soon have too many slaves and not enough land, whereas most people seemed to have too much land and not enough slaves.

One day after they had planted the last of the rice and she could afford no more seed, she was working on her long-neglected flowers when she stopped for a minute and looked at the sky. It had turned a sullen gray, and the air seemed almost touchable, as if poised for quick electric movement; but it was actually deathly still, hushing the movement of branches in the trees and seeming almost too heavy to be breathed properly. Puzzled and concerned at this oddity, she saw Moses come running in from the fields. He cried, "Miz Mad'lun, hurricane comin'! Blow ev-erthang away!"

Madeleine thought she could bear no more. "Oh no, not after all this work. The rice has not been planted long enough or deep enough. It will blow away for sure. If it does, I hope I blow away with it."

"Don't talk that way, Miz Mad'lun. Git in the tater cellar quick. I gits Lying Boy and the women."

Out of some sense of survival, Madeleine obeyed him. Moving slowly, she gathered up water, food, and a lantern and descended the steps from the kitchen to the potato cellar, dug by Moses only this summer. She sat in the cool dark, not bothering to light the lantern, until the others joined her. They had all been through hurricanes and were nervous, but Madeleine, who had never experienced one, did not seem to care. She did not speak the remainder of that day and all that night while the wind howled and screamed outside. They could hear the branches from the trees beat against the sides of the house. At one point they felt something solid bang against one wall. They felt the house shake and rattle and feared it would be nothing but a pile of lumber and bricks when the storm ended.

Madeleine hugged herself and rocked back and forth. She was too despondent even to pray. She knew her rice crop would never survive this; it was planted too shallow. Forgetting her dreams of a plantation, could she and her people survive with only the forty acres left that the Company would allow them? Her four companions, out of respect for her, did not speak either. Rima went through the motions of fingering her rosary beads, but omitted the usual accompanying chant.

Finally, as dawn was breaking, they emerged tentatively from the cellar. Some shutters were hanging from the windows, and a few boards missing from the roof, but the house was intact. Madeleine thanked God that they had fortified the house with brick. When they went outside, they found bushes and trees uprooted. One young magnolia tree had been blown up onto the roof of the house and hung there precariously. But the older magnolia trees and many of those planted last summer still stood.

Rima moaned and ran to the place where their new cabin had stood. The boards and their few belongings were scattered all the way down the hill. Moses and Madeleine, beginning to come out of her depression, tried to comfort her. Laff patted her hand and tried to lead her into the lean-to, indicating that she and Moses could stay there, but Madeleine intervened. "*Non*, you must not worry. You and Moses will stay in the smaller bedroom off the kitchen until we build you another cabin. I promise you it will be built long before the baby comes."

After Rima cheered up a little, Madeleine started walking through her fields. Her corn would have to be replanted; most of the stalks had been uprooted. The rest of her crops would probably be all right; they were either too deeply rooted or not far enough up for the wind to blow away. It was too soon to tell how many of the rice seeds had blown away. She would have to wait until the plants came up. She could see that the field had been damaged, for many of the rows had flattened from the wind.

As she walked back to the house, she began to recover and adjust. If a small farm were all they would ever have, it would be the best small farm on the Mississippi River. She would find out what crops yielded the best return and plant them. She began to make mental notes of the repairs that needed to be made. She tried to convince herself that she was resigned to losing the eighty acres to the Company.

A few weeks later she and Klaus checked her rice field to see how many seeds had survived the hurricane. Klaus and most of the other people in the area had planted earlier than Madeleine, so their crops had time to take root and therefore survived the storm. As they walked through the field, they saw that, as they had expected, at least half the crop had been blown away. The plants were coming up about twice as far apart as they had been planted. Madeleine tried not to show her disappointment. After all, she had known what to expect, but Klaus did not try to comfort her as she would have expected. He kept walking past the rice field and over the hill to her uncultivated land. She could see only the top of his blond head bobbing over the hill. Then she heard his loud, full-bellied laugh. "Madeleine, come look!"

Madeleine ran over the hill and saw him sitting on the ground, bent over howling with laughter. She thought he had taken leave of his senses. At best, he was not showing much sensitivity to her loss.

"Klaus, have you gone mad? What are you laughing at?"

"Look, Madeleine! Look as far as the eye can see. What do you see?"

Madeleine decided to humor him. "I see empty fields, with some rice growing here and there." The words echoed in her head: *with rice growing*! "Klaus, why is rice growing on uncultivated fields?"

"*Mein Gott*, you have been blessed. The hurricane did it. The wind blew it off your planted fields and scattered it over these unplanted ones. Now you have a huge, instant rice crop."

"But, Klaus, it is the same amount of rice. It is simply scattered over more acreage. It won't yield any more rice. It just means more land to cover during harvesting."

"*Ja*, more land to harvest—because you have more land under cultivation."

Madeleine felt almost afraid to grasp what he was saying. She repeated numbly, "More land under cultivation."

Klaus shook her. "Think, Madeleine, the ordinance for land grants does not say how well or by what manner the land is cultivated, just that it must be cultivated. The hurricane has saved you some more land."

Madeleine finally allowed herself to believe what he was saying. "Oh, Klaus! Oh, Klaus!" Usually undemonstrative, she surprised him by hugging his head to her waist, almost toppling him over. Then she picked up one end of her skirt with one hand, lifted the other hand to the sky and danced around a new rice plant.

At that moment Moses and Lying Boy, topping the hill after hearing the commotion, saw Klaus sitting and laughing and Madeleine dancing in the middle of the field. Moses thought Madeleine had gone mad from grief. Lying Boy thought she had been comforting herself with liquor. She explained what happened, and they did their own dance, careful not to stamp on a rice plant.

When the four of them walked off the acreage of hurricane-planted rice, they found it stretched to forty acres. In many places the rice was sparsely planted; but, as Klaus had said, it needed only to be planted to be considered under cultivation. That put eighty acres under cultivation. When an accounting was made in the fall, the West Indies Company allowed them another twenty acres, leaving one hundred acres in all, still enough to be considered a plantation instead of a farm. Madeleine had lost only twenty acres.

Chapter 24

Jacques stayed away from Magnolia Grove all that summer. He was fighting Indians most of this time, but he preferred to spend his free time in New Orleans. Madeleine saw him only once in August when she accompanied the Muellers into town to sell her produce. Moses did the actual selling and proved an effective salesman. What wasn't sold at market, he put into a cart and pulled it through Decatur Street to the rows of soldiers' barracks and sang out his wares in a loud cheerful voice.

"Come and gittum, soldiers, I got green peppers, snap-beans, tur-nips! I got oranges! I got celery! I got fine ripe yellow banana! Ba-na-na!"

With all the extra soldiers in town, especially with the influx of hearty-eating Swiss soldiers, there never seemed to be enough fresh vegetables and fruit. As soon as they heard Moses come up the street, they flocked to him, buying him out in a matter of minutes. Madeleine discovered

170

that they were willing to pay higher prices for some items, especially when the temptation was put under their noses. Sometimes she had Moses take only one popular item to barracks row.

"Watermelon, soldier! Come and git your nice red watermelon, soldier! I got melon with the water, red to the rind!"

Or another time he would call out, "Blackber-reees! Fresh and fine. I got blackber—reees, Soldier! Fresh from th' vine! I got blackberries, soldier! BLACK-BERRIEE-EEEEES!"

Moses became a permanent weekly fixture in New Orleans, appearing every Sunday with the Germans and leaving with them. He became something of a celebrity, known not only for his fresh produce but also for his distinctive street cries and his colorful clothing. Madeleine started dressing him in bright colors to attract more attention to him. Soon, of course, he had competition. Other plantation owners put their slaves into the streets to peddle their surplus produce until most days the streets rang out with their songs and cries. But Moses was the original, the one people bought from first. The soldiers especially remained loyal to him, because he was the first one to bring his produce directly to them.

Sometimes Lying Boy accompanied Moses to help him carry more food in a second pushcart. People were reluctant to buy from an Indian, even a friendly Choctaw, during this period of unrest, so he remained as unnoticeable as possible, tagging along behind Moses. Left on his own, Lying Boy would change the price of an item according to his whim. Or he might give away a bushel of potatoes if the mood struck him. His major contribution was his versatile voice. He could mimic Moses so well that most people could not tell the difference. That meant, when Moses's voice tired, Lying Boy could take over without anyone noticing. Sometimes they cried out in unison or in overlapping cries, interweaving lines rhythmically, making a unique duet.

Few people in New Orleans knew that Moses was hawking the proud Madeleine de Mandeville Bouligny's produce. When those people who did know asked Jacques about it, he was embarrassed and replied that they allowed Moses to do this to have a little income on his own. Then, after so many other plantation owners followed suit, he stopped being embarrassed and sometimes intercepted Lying Boy for a share of the profits, or a *loan* as he called it. Moses soon learned to keep all the money hidden in the bottom of one of the pushcarts. Jacques considered Moses more Madeleine's slave than his, so he was too ashamed to press the matter with him.

Jacques was becoming a bit desperate about his gambling debts. Something about him—his arrogant carriage, his charming wit, or perhaps his reputation for dueling—prevented his debtors from pressing him. Jean Claude Chauvin especially seemed willing to lend him money without pushing him for repayment. Jacques suspected that Chauvin relished his old rival for Madeleine's hand being indebted to him, but Jacques couldn't seem to stop himself from gambling. It provided excitement when he was off-duty.

He was finding that, though no one pressed him for money, people were beginning to avoid gambling with him, making excuses or forgetting to tell him where a game was being held. It had gotten to the point that some bars refused to let him join the card games. Up to this point he had kept his debtors satisfied by paying them a little every time he received his soldier's pay or his small stipend from his family. But he had gotten too far behind for this to mollify them. He knew he had to ask Madeleine for money, and he hated the idea.

As much as he despised the truth of it, he had to admit that he could not provide for her. He had gradually become aware that this farming scheme of hers was more than a hobby. She knew what she was doing, and she was more successful than she had indicated to him. He had heard from Perier that most of their land would be saved from reverting to the West Indies Company, but the news made him angry and resentful. He also felt guilty that Madeleine had to work so hard. He liked to think of her as a protected, even cosseted lady.

"Some lady!" he snorted to himself as he walked toward the Parraults' where he had heard she was visiting for the afternoon while her produce was being sold. "What lady would grub in the dirt during the hottest months every year?"

As he walked into the Parraults' parlor, Madeleine noticed that his drinking and late hours showed very little on him. His body was still trim and wiry, his face still handsome. Only the dark shadows under his eyes revealed his sleepless nights. Madeleine was glowing with health and vitality, her skin lightly tanned from the sun in spite of her careful attempts at protection. She was wearing a new dress for the occasion, for she had hoped she would see him that day. It was a light blue cotton cut simply to show off her long, lean body, now a little more filled out from Rima's good cooking. Her hair was brushed to a glossy shine, pulled up into a loose bun. She wore the de Mandeville brooch at her neck and looked every inch the aristocrat to Jacques.

They greeted each other like polite strangers, each lightly brushing the other on the cheek. Anne Parrault took her children for an afternoon of visiting so the young couple could be alone.

"Madeleine, you are looking more relaxed and confident than I have ever seen you. Prosperity suits you."

"*Merci*, Jacques, I have been lucky. I suppose you heard how the storm and the rice crop saved most of our land."

"*Oui*, everyone in New Orleans has heard about it. It is said that even the hurricanes bend to your will."

Madeleine ignored his sarcasm. "How have you been, Jacques?"

Jacques answered uneasily, "Actually I have been having some financial problems. I need two favors. Fortunately, I understand you have become wealthy enough to help me."

Madeleine was apprehensive. "I, we, are not wealthy, Jacques. The farm made just enough to see us all through the winter and for seed money and a few improvements next spring."

Jacques obviously did not believe her and said in an offhand manner, "Then I may need to sell some of the land. I don't want my wife to have to be responsible for that much land anyway."

Madeleine blanched. "You cannot do that. If it had not been for my work you would not have the land to sell. Oh, Jacques, why do you continue gambling?"

Jacques flushed with anger. "It is not for a wife to tell her husband how to live. Perhaps if my wife stayed at my side, I would not need to amuse myself gambling."

Madeleine knew it would be fruitless to remind him that he could not afford to keep her at his side. "How much money do you need?" she asked wearily.

When he mumbled the amount, her mouth dropped open in shock, "Jacques, how could you have lost that much? Do you really think I have that much money?"

"When I've had a little too much to drink, I sometimes wager too much. Madeleine, I know you have more money than you have been admitting to. I've seen Moses and Lying Boy peddling every week, and they do very well. Look, if you will just pay off my debts, I promise not to gamble again. I will spend most of this summer on the farm with you."

Madeleine did not believe that he would stop gambling. She knew, if she gave him her seed money, they would eventually lose the land. She was terrified about his threat to sell it. Then an idea occurred to her on how to protect the land. For a minute she tried to push it out of her mind, for she knew it would finish off her marriage. It would end any pretense that she was the protected wife and he the provider. She made up her mind: she admitted to herself that she would rather save the land than the marriage. The land she could count on, have some control over; the marriage she could not. The land bore fruit; the marriage did not. She began hesitantly, "I might be able to find most of the money," she saw the relief on Jacques' face. "But only on one condition."

"Does my wife intend to bargain with me?" Jacques said sarcastically, thinking she would ask for his promise not to gamble again.

"Yes, I do intend to bargain," she said firmly. "I will

give you the money if you sell me the land."

"If I what? You would have me sell my land to my own wife? Absolutely not! I would be a laughingstock." Jacques turned his back on her to keep from hitting her. How dare she make such a suggestion?

"You could tell people it was a gift because I love Magnolia Grove so much. Please, Jacques, it would still be your land too. It is only that I am afraid you will wager it in a game some night when you have had too much to drink. You said yourself that you sometimes act unwisely under those conditions." Madeleine tried to be conciliatory.

Jacques gripped her shoulders until she winced. "And what do I tell myself when I put my only property in my wife's hands—when I allow my wife to provide for us? Tell me that, my fine lady. Or are you really a fine lady?"

"What do you mean?" Madeleine asked shakily, knowing what he meant.

"I mean, what are you really? I know you are not a lady. A lady does not enjoy digging in the dirt. A lady does not drive such a sharp bargain with her husband that it is like a stake in his heart. Who are you?" He shook her until her hair fell from its bun.

Madeleine answered in a resigned voice, "If you will kindly release me, I will tell you." He took his hands from her shoulders, recoiling from the fine tendrils of hair clinging to his fingers.

She continued, "My name was Madeleine Boucher. I was a maid in the de Mandeville home, and my father was a serf on their estate. The clerk made a mistake with my name on the ship, so I decided to take advantage of his error. I was tired of being treated like a servant, and I did not want to marry a servant."

Jacques shook his head in disbelief. "So you tricked *me* into marrying a servant. And you acquired an aristocratic name of your own for real. Now you want my land too! How do you reconcile that with your religion you are so serious about?"

Madeleine could not answer. She looked away from his accusing eyes.

Jacques continued to lash out at her. "You said you didn't want to be treated like a servant, yet you are willing to work like one. You are willing to peddle your onions and potatoes like one."

Now it was Madeleine's turn to feel blinding rage. "Willing, yes! Desiring, no! I would have preferred to act the fine lady and sit with my friends drinking *café au lait*. I would like to occupy my time buying pretty clothes. I would like to care for my husband and my home and a child. After all, I lied to get that kind of life, did I not?"

Jacques examined his boots, but Madeleine gave no quarter. "Why didn't I occupy myself with these pleasant, *ladylike* activities? Because my *gentleman* husband was not home. As a matter of fact, I *had* no home. I had no child. And I had no money for pretty clothes, or even for *café au lait*. Faced with the choice of starving in a genteel manner or laboring like a servant, I chose to work. That is still my choice!"

"Madeleine, you know I would not have let you starve, and you know the farm has become more than a means of providing you food and clothing. It is not a farm to you; it is a plantation—Magnolia Grove. I hate that pretentious name! It is a fraud, just as you are."

Madeleine said with quiet determination, "I will make it a plantation the same way I made myself a lady."

"You may make that farm into a plantation; it is only dirt, after all. But you cannot make yourself into a lady. A lady is born, not made. And, *ma cherie*, the peasant in you is very near to the surface."

Madeleine said wearily, "Perhaps you are right about that. There is no point in arguing. There are some things we cannot change. Let us work on the problems that can be solved. Do you agree to sell me the land?"

Jacques looked at her as if to measure her determination. "You know I could take the money from you and keep the land too. What belongs to you belongs to me."

"You could if you could find the money. But you won't do that. You are too much of a gentleman, *n'est-ce pas?*"

"Very well, you win. I could not do that. You may have the land, but I now have a condition."

"What condition?" Madeleine asked warily, uneasy at the vengeful look in his eyes.

Jacques had no opportunity to answer her. They were interrupted by loud voices outside. They rushed out and saw a crowd heading for the levee just in front of town. "What is going on?" Jacques asked a soldier he knew in the crowd.

"Come watch the fun, Captain. Six Natchez Indians have been captured. Governor Perier is going to make a public example of them."

Madeleine started to go back into the house. "Jacques, I do not want to see them punished. Let's finish our talk."

Jacques took her arm firmly and half pulled her along with him to the levee. "*Non*, I want you to watch this. It will make finishing our talk much easier."

Madeleine looked at him curiously and went with him, unwilling to be seen openly quarreling. When they reached the levee and Jacque maneuvered them into a place at the front of the crowd, they saw Governor Perier standing on the levee in front of six Indians under heavy guard. Madeleine was surprised to see not six fierce Natchez warriors, but only two young warriors, two old men, and two women. Surely, she thought, Governor Perier did not mean to punish all of them. The old men and women could not have made war on anyone.

Governor Perier made a long speech about the massacre at Fort Rosalie and how he had rescued the captives and chased off the Natchez. He said, "We will never be safe until we have ferreted out every Natchez and destroyed him. They will grow stronger and increase in number until they come back and murder us in our beds."

The crowd began to grow restless, so Perier finally stopped talking and gave a signal to the guards. Madeleine watched in fascinated horror as they tied the prisoners to six stakes and spread dry leaves and corn shucks around them. She turned away and tried to leave, but Jacques stopped her. "I want you to see this."

"Why? It is inhuman what they are doing."

"You will understand in good time. Watch!" he ordered.

Madeleine watched as Perier gave a slight nod to a soldier with a torch. The soldier set fire to the leaves and corn shucks, and the flames started to lick at the Indians' feet. Madeleine watched their faces, frozen, whether from courage or fear she did not know. They made no sound, neither pleading nor cursing. The fire leapt up and crackled around their legs. First it consumed their clothes, then their flesh. The air was filled with an odd, sweet, burnt smell. Still there was no sound from the Indians. Just before Madeleine finally looked away, she saw the expression on one of the women's faces. Her eyes were glazed with pain; her face was contorted in agony, but she still made no sound.

Madeleine tore herself out of Jacques's grasp then and ran to the Parraults' on weak, trembling legs. He followed her and gently put her to bed. Madeleine could not stop shaking. She knew the memory of that woman was permanently etched in her memory.

"Jacques, why did you want me to see that? Do you hate me so much?"

"*Non*, Madeleine, it is because of what I will show you tomorrow. We will finish our conversation then. Rest now. I will be back in the morning."

Madeleine closed her eyes but knew she would not sleep.

Chapter 25

The morning after the public burning of the Natchez, Jacques called for Madeleine at the Parraults' as he had promised. Madeleine, having slept very little, was ready, dressed in her old faded blue dress, the same one she was wearing when she arrived in New Orleans. Her hair was pulled back tightly in its usual twist.

Jacques and Madeleine walked without speaking for more than an hour. They were soon out of New Orleans and into the woods south of the town. Madeleine became more and more curious as they walked through areas more and more isolated. Her pride would not allow her to question him. She noted that he made no pretense of thinking she was too delicate to walk such a long distance. Nor did he take her arm when she stumbled. So much for gallantry, she thought wryly.

He stopped when they came to a cave almost hidden by bushes. Madeleine watched in amazement as the bushes moved and then parted. Appearing in front of them was a lovely young Indian girl. As she moved forward a few more steps, Madeleine noticed that she limped slightly. She looked as if she had not eaten well in some time; her face was gaunt and her arms were thin. But her breasts were full, and her belly was rounded.

Madeleine looked from her to Jacques and back again. Realization dawned in her eyes. "Who is this, Jacques?" she asked, knowing already more than she wanted to.

Without expression, Jacques answered as if he were introducing her at a party. "This is Lame Doe. She is a Natchez princess, sister of Great Sun, chief of the Natchez. It was her mother, Pricked Arm, who warned me about the massacre at Fort Rosalie."

Madeleine avoided asking the more important question. "Why is she here? She is obviously in danger. Why did she not flee with her people?"

"She and her mother, Pricked Arm, were left behind because of their part in warning me. Her mother did not want to live so she starved herself to death. I have been hiding Lame Doe here since spring, but it is getting too dangerous. There are more and more scouting expeditions. They are certain to find her."

Since spring, Madeleine thought; then she must be about four or five months pregnant. Finally, Madeleine could avoid asking no longer. "Why did you bring me here? What can I do? Why must you involve me? I don't want to know about this."

Jacques played his trump card then, "This is the other condition for selling you the land."

"*Non*, Jacques, please. Do not ask me. It is too cruel."

Jacques would not look at her and said with some

sincerity, "I am sorry, Madeleine. I know of no other way. She will die if she stays here. You saw what happened to the Natchez prisoners yesterday. Do you want that to happen to her?"

Madeleine wanted to scream, "Yes, burn her! Burn her!" But she could not. In a resigned voice, she instead asked, "What do you want me to do?"

"Take her back with you to the farm. Pass her off as a Choctaw, as a cousin perhaps of Lying Boy's from another tribe."

Without much hope, Madeleine tried to convince him of the absurdity of this plan. "And what about her hair and her clothes and her language? Does she never speak? Is she willing to live her whole life without speaking? She would be recognized as Natchez immediately."

Jacques said eagerly, "I have thought of that. You can change her hair and give her some of Laff's clothes. And you can teach her Choctaw. She already knows some French. She knows she can never speak Natchez again."

"And the baby, Jacques, am I to take care of the baby too? Am I to teach it? Do I teach it to be Indian or white?"

Jacques reached out as if to touch her arm. "I am sorry, Madeleine. That is my condition for selling you the land. With the improvements you have made, I could get a good price from someone else and send her to Canada."

Madeleine knew she had no choice. Her face hardened into a look Jacques had never seen her wear before. "I agree. Have the papers drawn up, and I will bring the money with me next market day."

All this time the Indian girl had stood without speaking, looking straight ahead. Madeleine had no idea how much of the conversation she understood. She instructed

Jacques in a cold, impersonal voice, "Stay with her and have her ready in a few hours. Lying Boy and I will pick her up in his pirogue."

Unable to look at either of them again, she left and walked back to town alone. She had walked for half an hour when she had to stop and sit on a log. Her shoulders heaved with dry sobs.

Later that day Madeleine was riding back to Magnolia Grove with two silent Indians, Lying Boy and Lame Doe. Lying Boy for once was surprised into speechlessness. Madeleine began to laugh hysterically. Here I am, she thought, taking care of a pregnant woman by my husband, and I cannot get pregnant myself. Lying Boy stared at his mistress and laughed politely with her, not understanding the joke.

Chapter 26

Six years had passed since Madeleine first arrived in New Orleans. It was now 1734 and the town had grown considerably. Governor Perier had been replaced by former Governor Bienville, who inherited the same Indian problems. Jacques still was away a lot fighting Indians. He was beginning to show signs of his nightlife: his eyes had become puffy and he had lines of dissatisfaction etched around his mouth.

Magnolia Grove was now a small but thriving plantation. Madeleine had increased her rice crop and bought a mule, a cow, and a bull from her German neighbors. She had been lucky to get them. Livestock was so rare in Louisiana that there was still a law, now on punishment of death, against killing them. She had added another cabin for Lying Boy and Laff, plus another room to the main house so she could have a parlor. But she deliberately limited her expansion to protect herself and Jacques. She knew that, if Jacques suspected how well she was really doing, he would gamble even more. As it was, she regularly had to pay enough on his debts to keep his creditors away, though discreetly, of course. She also tried to protect his pride by not seeming too successful. If she were honest with herself, she had to admit that she also had not given up the dream of living like a lady someday.

Madeleine and Jacques had become like polite strangers or like business partners. They made token visits with each other. In the past five years, Jacques had rarely claimed his marital rights in bed and always in New Orleans, never at Magnolia Grove. Madeleine put her energies into her plantation in the spring and summer and in her religion and volunteer work in the fall and winter. Though she could now afford a small house in New Orleans, she continued to stay with the Parraults in their crowded house. She now left the servants at Magnolia Grove all year round.

Though Madeleine had children all around her, she was still childless. She was now twenty-five and despaired of ever having children. All her friends in New Orleans had children, even her enemies. Suzanne had one boy and two girls, but she was careful never to gloat about this to Madeleine, wisely remembering Madeleine's threat to reveal her miscarriage before she married. Marie O'Brien, Jacques's former mistress, also had two sturdy red-haired children, a boy and a girl. Madeleine often saw Marie strutting with her children at market, but the two women continued not to speak.

Magnolia Grove, it seemed to her, had doubled as a nursery. Rima and Moses had two boys, while poor Laff had died giving birth to a boy. Lying Boy, she remembered, had been inconsolable. He would not talk for a year except to answer in short grunts. Then he consoled himself with Lame Doe, whose own son, fathered by Jacques, was born dead. Madeleine remembered that night with mixed emotions. Lame Doe had stayed out of her sight while carrying Jacques's child. She had been staying in Lying Boy's and Laff's cabin and then, at Madeleine's insistence, in Rima's after Laff died. It was from that cabin that Madeleine had heard Lame Doe's animal-like cries all the way into her bedroom.

Finally, unable to bear the noises any longer, she got up and ran to their cabin just in time to see Rima deliver Lame Doe's stillborn boy, choked to death by the umbilical cord. When Lame Doe saw the baby and then Madeleine in the doorway, she turned her face to the wall without a word. Madeleine tried not to look at the dark-haired lifeless infant—quickly covered by Rima, who had noticed its white skin—and rushed out of the room. She could not help but feel some relief that she would not have to see that child grow up on Magnolia Grove. Her dreams that night turned to nightmares, filled with images of fetuses and dead babies and the sound of Suzanne Chauvin's laughter.

Lame Doe recovered her health quickly and nursed Laff's baby from her milk-laden breasts. Little by little, she took complete charge of the baby, called Strong Bear, and of Lying Boy, finally moving in with them, in spite of Madeleine's protests. Before long, Lame Doe and Lying Boy had their own son, whom they later called Fleet Deer because he was always trying to run away from them into the woods. When this baby was born, Madeleine insisted that they observe a simple wedding ceremony.

Madeleine then had four growing boys to teach and love and look forward to their helping her on the farm. When she had told Jacques about Lame Doe's son being born dead, he seemed to share her relief, though he made no comment. The barriers between them stayed up, but she got the impression that he regretted foisting off this particular problem onto her. It had been difficult for her and her small family of servants to get used to Lame Doe, but she had to admit that the Natchez Indian princess proved to be quiet and useful. Only the Muellers suspected that she was anything other than a distant relative of Lying Boy's. The girl improved her French with Madeleine's help, and she learned enough Choctaw words to allay any suspicions.

As it turned out, Madeleine's special thorn in the side was not Lame Doe, for Jacques stayed away from Lame Doe on his infrequent visits. Then, after Lying Boy took her for his woman, Madeleine knew she had nothing to worry about from her. She told herself that Jacques would never go near her again.

Madeleine's new burden came from an unexpected source, Rima's little girl, now two years old. The problems began even with her pregnancy. In contrast to her other pregnancies, Rima seemed unhappy with this one. She moped around and was sick a great deal of the time. Moses too seemed disinterested and listless. They did very little work that summer. Moses even refused to go to New Orleans to market. On the one occasion when Madeleine forced him, he would not sing out his street cries to sell the produce, so she sent Lying Boy in his place. Lying Boy was able to mimic Moses expertly, but people seemed to shy away from an Indian who could sound like a Negro peddler. It was a lean year; she barely broke even.

For the first time, Rima had a difficult delivery with that third baby, a breach birth, leaving her unable to have more children. When the baby was born with light chocolate skin, Madeleine thought she understood the problem. Naturally, she wondered if Jacques were the father but pushed that thought away. *Non,* he seldom comes near any of us and then only when he needs money. Even Jacques would not betray me with our servants twice.

She questioned Rima, whom she had grown to love. "Rima, tell me, who is the father of your baby?"

She answered sullenly, "Moses, Ma'am."

"No, Rima, Moses can't be the father. The baby's skin is too light. You and Moses are very dark. Besides, Moses won't come near this baby, and you know he loves his other children."

"I guess he don't like gal babies."

Madeleine admonished her gently, "I don't believe that. Now, you must tell me. The baby's father is white, isn't he?"

"Yessum."

"Did he rape you, Rima?"

"No'm, not zactly."

"What then exactly did he do? Would you tell me that?"

"No'm."

Madeleine began to get a little impatient. "Did it happen in New Orleans?"

"No'm."

"*Mon Dieu*, Rima, did it happen here at Magnolia Grove, when I went to New Orleans for the winter and left you and Moses here to look after the place?"

Rima was silent.

"Was it, it couldn't have been Klaus Mueller?"

"No'm," Rima said, for the first time with some emphasis.

"Very well," Madeleine said with some exasperation. "You are entitled to some privacy. But you must tell me if you think you might be taken advantage of again."

"Yessum," replied Rima impassively.

Madeleine did not question her again. The little girl was named Mary Claire, and everybody on the farm fussed over her except Rima and Moses. They took care of the child but did not cuddle her or even punish her as they did their boys. They remained troubled and remote, especially around Madeleine.

Mary Claire was a beautiful little girl with soft, curly dark hair and big velvety brown eyes. She started walking and talking much earlier than the other children. Madeleine gave her a great deal of attention and liked to pretend she was her own child. Even Jacques seemed to like the child. One day when he was visiting Magnolia Grove, he was swinging Mary Claire on the rope swing on the porch. He pushed her really high and she laughed aloud with delight. He laughed too and stopped the swing to put his face next to hers.

Madeleine rounded the corner of the house with a pail of blackberries she had just picked in time to see this scene. She stopped and dropped her pail of blackberries, dotting the grass with them. With ringing ears and blurry eyes, she bent over to pick them up, barely able to see them. She picked up as many rocks as she did blackberries. All she could see were those two thin, aristocratic faces side by side and those two slender hands next to each other on the rope.

No, Jacques, she thought. Not again, not with Rima. I was a fool not to admit it to myself the first time I saw Mary Claire's face.

Mary Claire jumped off the porch to help her pick up the blackberries. Madeleine gave her a shove and said sharply, "*Non*, I will do it. Leave me be!"

Mary Claire drew back immediately with a hurt, frightened look on her face. Her lips trembled, but she pressed them together to keep from crying. Over her head, Madeleine and Jacques looked at each other for a long time, without speaking. Jacques was the first to look away. He got on his horse and rode away, not returning for a long time.

Chapter 27

A year had passed since Madeleine found out about Mary Claire. She never again spoke harshly to the little girl, but she was no longer affectionate to her. For a long time Mary Claire would forget that Madeleine had changed and run eagerly up to her, only to be politely rebuffed. Finally, she no longer ran up to her.

Fortunately for Mary Claire, once Rima realized that Madeleine knew who Mary Claire's father was, some of the burden of guilt seemed to lift and she started showing the child more affection. Then Moses seemed to get used to her and started acting more like her father. Relations between Madeleine and Rima remained strained.

Magnolia Grove no longer was a place of refuge for Madeleine. She felt doomed to live here with one after another of Jacques's former mistresses—or victims. All she needed now was Marie O'Brien or perhaps even Suzanne Chauvin to move in with her, she thought bitterly. She did her work mechanically, for she knew she could make no further expansions or major improvements without seeming ambitious and masculine. She had not seen Jacques in a year, not since that day she found out that he was Mary Claire's father. She knew now that she would never have children and brooded about it more than ever.

She became listless and had trouble sleeping. She lost her appetite. Rima outdid herself preparing delicacies to tempt her. One day she made a blackberry cobbler, and Madeleine left the table without eating anything. Rima did not know that Madeleine hated the sight of blackberries since that afternoon she had found out about Mary Claire.

Rima began to fuss over her more and more, as she used to; but Madeleine did not respond. One morning Rima came in the house and discovered that Madeleine had not gotten dressed. She was sitting in her nightgown, rocking back and forth in her rocking chair. In her arms she held Mary Claire's corn-shuck doll that Moses had fashioned for the child.

"Miz Mad'lun, here now, you cain't be actin' like this. You got to git up and go on. It ain't like you to lay down on the job."

"What does it matter, Rima? What is the work for? I have no children to leave anything to. I will never have children." She laughed bitterly, "How can I? My husband won't come near me. He prefers anybody *but* me." Then she realized what she had said and looked up at Rima.

The two women looked at each other directly for the first time in a year. They looked for a long time and simultaneously reached out and clasped each other's hands tightly. Even in her fog, Madeleine was aware that Rima would never have initiated any intimacy with Jacques and that their union was partly her own fault for not warming her husband's bed. Then Rima took charge and played mistress. She told Madeleine what clothes to put on and what chores to do to keep her busy. When Madeleine was too preoccupied to think, Rima went out to the field and told Moses, "You got to go to New Orleans and fetch Mr. Jacques. Miz Mad'lun need him. Bring him back tonight, you hear. Don't come back without him."

Just before dark that night, before Moses returned with Jacques, Rima said to Madeleine, "Here, Miz Mad'lun. Put on your shawl. We goin' to walk in the woods. There somebody I want you to see. She help you."

Madeleine got up and followed her obediently. She did not seem to care where she went. They walked for an hour past the small swamp on Madeleine's land and deep into the woods, farther than Madeleine had ever been before. At last they reached a cove where a few cabins and tents were clustered. She saw only women, no men or children. The women looked different from the usual slaves Madeleine was familiar with. They seemed stronger, sleeker. Instead of the customary chignon wrapped about their hair, usually worn by women of color, these women wore their hair bushy and free, decorated with bones or beads.

Rima nodded to them as if she knew them and took Madeleine into the largest cabin, though sparsely furnished. In front of a blazing fire with several overhanging pots stood a wizened-looking old woman with almond shaped eyes. "Mattie," Rima said, "I brung you somebody needs your help. I owe her. She need a baby."

Madeleine looked around and saw strange vials and exotic smelling, unrecognizable substances all around her. She felt the old woman's eyes on her and was a little frightened. She got up as if to leave, but Mattie seemed to draw her back with her will power.

She spoke to Madeleine soothingly, "Now jes' you relax, honey. We gone fix you up." Madeleine sat back down.

Then Mattie turned to Rima. "Rima, you go tell the others to get everything ready. I'll mix the potion." She dipped into one of the pots boiling in the fireplace and added substances from some of the vials on a shelf.

"Drank this, honey; it will make you feel better." Madeleine obeyed and found it to be a sweet, but not cloying, warm liquid that seemed to radiate heat all the way down. Madeleine felt more relaxed, almost dreamlike. Her limbs lost their stiffness and felt loose and limber. She was not sure how much time had passed when Mattie told her to get up and led her gently outside.

A circle of women was seated around a fire right beside a small waterfall that splashed softly into a spring. Madeleine sat down beside Rima and grinned. "I feel wonderful, Rima!"

Rima smiled back at her. "You gone feel a whole lot better, Miz Madeleine."

Mattie brought a large gourd of a steaming liquid to the circle and passed it around. Each woman took a sip and passed it on. When it was Madeleine's turn to sip, Rima took it from her and passed it to the next person. "You don't need this, Miz Mad'lun, we got somethin' special for you."

Madeleine did not argue; she sat and watched and listened. She didn't think she would ever argue or get upset about anything again. She felt at peace. And, as Rima had promised, they did have something special for her. Mattie gave her a handful of unfamiliar smelling seeds to chew.

How odd, she thought, but she obediently chewed the bitter-tasting seeds and began to feel as if she were floating on a cloud. She felt weightless; yet she had never felt more clearheaded and aware of her body. She had an overwhelming desire to touch her body parts. She started with the neck and stroked gently, enjoying the fine, smooth texture of her skin. She lightly ran her fingers over her breasts, waist, and thighs. She began to feel a slow liquid heat run through her body. She wished she could pull off her clothes and feel the heat of the fire on her body, then giggled at the thought.

Mattie picked up a drum and started to beat a slow, soft rhythm. The women hummed in tune with the drumbeat and started a slow, sinuous dance around the fire. At first Madeleine just sat and swayed a little in time with the rhythm. Then she felt irresistibly drawn to the circle of dancing women and joined a primitive, sensual dance that she seemed to have known all her life.

She and the other women moved their bodies like snakes, as if they had no bones. Madeleine was aware of her body as never before. The heat within her continued to burn. As the drum beat faster, the humming turned into a musical blend of shouts, and the women moved faster and faster. They stamped their feet, thrust their pelvises forward, and shook their upper bodies. Madeleine's hair came loose and fell about her face and shoulders. It felt like silk on her face; she turned her head this way and that to better feel her hair slide over her skin, over her nipples.

She lifted her hands to the full moon as the other women were doing, flung back her head, and danced even more frantically. She felt as if every part of her body was in motion. Then the drum slowed again, and the dancing slowed with it.

The circle of women straightened out and formed a line of still-moving bodies dancing toward the stream. Without speaking, as each woman got to the water's edge, she pulled off her clothes and waded in. Madeleine was fascinated as each strong, supple black body bared itself in the moonlight. She could hardly wait for her turn. Still moving to the drumbeat, she slipped out of her clothes with great relief. The air felt crisp and clean. The soft pout of her nipples disappeared and became rigidly erect; she thrust them out proudly and examined them with her hands as if she had never seen them before.

When she walked into the water, she became aware of her body in a new way. The water lapped about her slender legs and buttocks. As the water caressed her hips, the heat intensified so that the water could not have cooled them if it had turned to ice. She bent her knees and felt the water lap around her breasts. She ran her hands around and around her breasts, brushing her nipples with her fingertips.

She was so absorbed in her pleasure that she had almost forgotten the other women until Rima took her by the hand and led her to the waterfall. "Rima, what a beautiful body you have! No wonder Jacques wanted you!" Her own voice seemed as rich and smooth and slow as molasses; it poured sweetly out of her mouth. She stuck out her tongue and ran the tip over her lips to see if she could taste her voice.

Rima led her to the waterfall, and Madeleine lifted her face and arms up to meet the cool water faintly stinging her skin. Madeleine had never felt so refreshed, so alive, yet so relaxed at the same time. It was as if she had been bathed inside and out by water and light and air.

Then Rima led her out from under the waterfall. Madeleine's hair streamed to her waist, plastered to her body. She noticed that the other women were bathing themselves and each other. She watched with fascination as a young, slender woman lathered the full pendulous breasts of a larger one. The soap glistened on the dark skin. Madeleine could not take her eyes from a small bubble hanging precariously on a large nipple. She pursed her lips as if to blow the bubble away. Though she was too far away to have any effect, the bubble burst at that moment and left the wet, erect nipple free. As the woman tried to shake herself dry, her flesh jiggled madly, her huge breasts seemingly dancing in midair. Madeleine fancied that they moved to the beat of the still-pounding drum.

Rima and another woman started to lather Madeleine with a lilac scented soap. She surrendered to their touch. It was like having two mothers bathing her. She looked at her own white body between the two black ones, amazed at the contrast. For the first time, her slim, boyish body seemed beautiful to her.

Rima led her back under the waterfall to rinse the soap off her body. Then she and the other women returned to the fire. This time Madeleine was in the center of the circle. She had thought nothing could feel better than the water gently lapping at her naked body, but she had to admit that the fire drying and warming her felt even better. When she was completely dry, the women, two at a time, rubbed scented oil into her skin. Each oil seemed to have a different scent. The drumbeats became as soft as the flutter of a butterfly's wing. Madeleine concentrated on the scents as she felt the strong fingers massaging her body. The first was clove, yes, clove, then lilac again, then rose, then what, oh pine, maybe, then one she didn't recognize. It was almost like her own secret musk. It smelled best of all.

The hands kept massaging and rubbed every place on her body, came near its recesses but moved teasingly on. She closed her eyes and imagined these were men's hands touching her. She felt Jacques's hands, then Captain Beauchamp's, then Klaus Mueller's, then Governor Perier's, then Jacques's again. How could she have thought his touching her was unpleasant? If only he would touch her like this.

Just when the golden-red light in her body burned too hot to bear any longer and her torso began to writhe, the hands dropped away. Oh no, she thought, my skin is so lonely without being touched. See how my breasts reach out to be touched. She moaned in disappointment when her clothes were put on her. As Rima led her away, she looked back at the dark bodies glowing by the fire.

When Rima and Madeleine returned home, Moses was serving Jacques his supper. They both looked up and stared as the two women entered the kitchen. Moses shook his head as he saw Rima's damp, kinky hair and the self-satisfied look in her eyes. But it was Madeleine that made their eyes nearly pop out. Her hair was damp also, but what really shocked them was the fact that it flowed unbound down her back, a few tendrils wafting toward one breast. Her dress too was slightly damp and clung to her body. She smiled at them radiantly and made a deep curtsy to Jacques, the same one that had charmed him so at the levee the day their courtship began.

"Jacques, I am so glad you are here. It is wonderful to see you. You look so handsome." She seemed to float across the room and kissed him warmly on the cheek, her soft lips gently grazing the side of his mouth, her scent tantalizing his nostrils.

Jacques pulled back in horror. It was even worse than Moses had said, he thought; she was completely out of her mind. "Where the hell have you been?"

"Not hell, *mon cher*, heaven!" she retorted.

Moses too demanded suspiciously of Rima, "Where you done take Miz Mad'lun?"

Rima replied calmly, "It was a warm night. Miz Mad'lun say she want to bathe in the river. So we done it. What's all the fuss about?"

Madeleine giggled girlishly, "Yes, we done it." Turning to Jacques, she asked him, "Did you get enough to eat? Is there anything else you want?"

Jacques looked at her suspiciously. She did seem all right, just different. If he didn't know better, he would swear she had been drinking. There was something about the way she moved, not her usual brisk, efficient movements but slow liquid ones. He watched as she stretched herself sensuously like a cat, her head and buttocks thrown back with her hair making a bridge between them. He cleared his throat uneasily as he noticed Moses watching her too.

Moses got the point immediately and grabbed Rima by the arm. "Well, we better get to our cabin and see to the kids. Come on, Rima."

Rima shook her arm loose and said, "First I got to fix Mr. Jacques a drink, a special hot drink before I goes. You go on ahead."

Moses pulled her aside before he left and hissed in her ear, "Woman, ain't you done enough harm this night? You done took Miz Mad'lun to the conjure woman, ain't you?"

Rima just smiled and said aloud, "Yes, honey, you go on now. I bring some sweet milk when I come."

She bustled around the kitchen, chattering companionably as she mixed a drink for Jacques. Madeleine just sat at the table, looked at Jacques, and hummed softly. Jacques looked from one to the other, then absentmindedly gulped the drink Rima handed him. He gasped, trying to get his breath, *"Mon Dieu*, this drink is strong. Rima, are you trying to poison me? What is this strange, sweet taste?"

"Just a little cloves to flavor it. Takes the bitter out. Don't you like it, Mr. Jacques? I fix you another, you don't like it."

"It's all right."

"I be goin' then. Good night, Mr. Jacques. Good night, Miz Mad'lun. Rest well."

Jacques grunted. Madeleine got up, walked her to the door, and said, *"Bonsoir*, Rima dear." Jacques stared in amazement.

Madeleine stood in the open doorway for a moment with the moonlight streaming in. It gave her hair blue highlights and made her skin look like fresh cream. She gave another one of those slow stretches, this time lifting her hair up as she raised her arms then letting her hair fall in a shimmering mass. She yawned delicately and said sleepily, "I think I will go to bed. Won't you join me?"

Jacques felt an immediate response to her words, then thought, no, she could not have meant the same bed. We have not shared the same bed in years. She is just tired. He sat there for a while enjoying the effects of the quiet summer night and savoring the drink. The more he drank the better it got. It gave him a warm, relaxed glow he had not felt in a long time. He must ask Rima how she mixed it.

He dreaded going to bed alone. He wished he and Madeleine were on better terms; she looked so soft and lovely tonight. Well, he must have had too much to drink. Inside, she was hard as flint and twice as sharp. He wondered why Moses had insisted that he come. She was in a strange mood, but obviously not in any difficulty.

He got up and made his way in the dark to the small guestroom. He pulled off his clothes and got into the small bed. As he slipped under the light blanket, he felt warm, soft flesh. "*Mon Dieu*, who in the devil is in my bed?"

"Jacques?" Madeleine said sweetly, "Jacques?"

Jacques reached out his arms automatically and she snuggled in, pressing her body gently, slowly, part by part, against his. Her flesh burned against his, igniting his own. She put her head on his shoulder, fanning her hair out over his chest. He lay there without moving, just feeling. His limbs seemed so heavy he felt he could not move them.

Madeleine moved enough for both of them. She was in constant motion. Her lips were against his cheeks, his ear, lightly teasing his eyebrows. Her hands were caressing his hair, his neck, his chest, his groin. She caressed him with her burning body. He reached up to touch her but had to let his hands drop from the effort. She brought her body to his hands. Her breast fell into his cupped hand. How soft and smooth it felt, he thought. Its nipple pushed through his fingers.

The soft down between her legs brushed against his legs. He strained toward her. He longed to move but still could not. Again, she came to him. She rose above him, her long hair falling on each side of her face forming a curtain around his.

Jacques simply could not believe, even in his dreamlike state, that this was his wife. He knew he must be dreaming when she lowered herself on him and gripped him with her strong legs. Then he could think no more; he surrendered himself to her and moved to her rhythm until she reached a feverish pitch of excitement and found release. Slowly, easily, he too climaxed and drew her to him wonderingly. They slept in each other's arms and then, almost in their sleep, made love again—effortlessly and naturally—and finally slept the sleep of the dead.

Part IV.
Back to New Orleans, 1742

Chapter 28

Once more Madeleine was going down the Mississippi River making her regular autumn move from Magnolia Grove to New Orleans. In the past eight years she had begun to skip several seasons of moving back to New Orleans for the winter and had stayed year-round at Magnolia Grove. She sat in the front of the pirogue barely looking back at the familiar scenes passing by; yet she couldn't help noting, with a sense of surprise and satisfaction, how the countryside had become more settled, more civilized. Woody, swampy areas of the delta were gradually coming under the control of man. Aside from increasing acreage under tillage at her own Magnolia Grove, she saw other cleared areas sprouting crops or cattle, some of them only a half-acre or so. Others were good-sized fields of ten acres cleared from the heavy growths of light timber along the shore of the river. Near the fields were houses, lean-tos, barns—all the trappings of farm life, different and less permanent somehow from those she remembered on farms in her native France. But they were good signs, she thought, of the order and stability from the wealth provided by the river and its generous delta.

The river itself, seeming so placid as the pirogue slid easily over its surface, was a dictator, in a way, to the human beings who had the courage and the temerity to build along its shores. Madeleine noted that most houses had to be built on high ground where floods could not reach, as she had insisted whenever they added buildings of any sort at Magnolia Grove. Here and there on land that swept upward from the water at a very slight angle, she could see great fans of driftwood and brush heaved ashore in the flood season. On some houses she saw horizontal green and brown stains at various levels that revealed the constant threatening grasp of the dominant river—the mighty Mississippi. Madeleine smiled to herself, as if identifying with the qualities of strength and subdued power that she sensed in the flow of those waters. The river, she thought, must be female, for it nurtured and supported yet remained ominous in its unpredictability.

Lying Boy sat in the middle, rowing, and chattered whenever a silence fell. This was not often because at the back of the pirogue was Solange, Madeleine's vivacious, seven-year-old daughter. Unlike her mother, who was lost in her own thoughts, Solange was looking around her curiously and commenting on everything she saw.

"I see a snake!" Solange suddenly shouted, breaking the quiet punctuated only by the soft slap of the water against the sides of the boat. "There it is." She pointed to the left and slightly ahead.

"That ain't no snake. Just a floating stick," said Lying

Boy.

"It is too a snake. I saw it move." Solange's voice was immediately combative, as if she had little tolerance for disagreement. "I know a snake when I see one, and that's a snake. I don't care what you say. Just watch and you'll see."

Lying Boy turned the boat slightly toward the form in the water, and as he did so the four-foot *stick* came to life— a cottonmouth moccasin, a deadly inhabitant of the area, more commonly found in the bayous than in the river itself. The snake seemed to look up at the people in the boat and then submerged rapidly and disappeared astern.

"You right, Miss Solange," he said. "I sure didn't think that was a snake, not way out here, but you never can tell about them cottons. You make sure you watch out for them even when you playin' around in the shallow water. They be everywhere around here." His advice was sound, for Solange had always loved the water. She sneaked off to go swimming in the river so often that finally Madeleine had assigned David, Rima's oldest son and an excellent swimmer, to go to the river with Solange and Mary Claire every day.

Madeline winced a bit as she listened to their talk, for Lying Boy's French was certainly not the correct school-French she had learned from the Countess de Mandeville and the nuns. It bothered her that Lying Boy could never get his pronouns straightened out. He used the familiar *tu* for everybody, never the more formal *vous* that employers and owners ought to be addressed by all the time.

"Reminds me," he went on, "of one time we hunt frogs down by that stream back of the dryin' sheds. I bent down to get a stick out of the shallow water near the bank. Just as I pick it up it moved and nearly bit my hand off. I picked it up by the tail and chucked it at a frog so hard it killed 'em both."

Solange and Madeleine exchanged knowing looks. Solange cooperatively exclaimed "Oooweee!" then went on to ask him questions about his story, even though she knew it was a fantasy.

Madeleine thought wearily that Solange was the only person she knew who could outtalk Lying Boy. She looked fondly at her curly dark-haired, sherry-eyed child and thought what a miracle it was that Solange had even been conceived. Madeleine blushed as she thought back to that night when she was so unlike herself. She could remember very little of what had happened, but she knew she must have been unforgivably bold because Jacques never came to her bed again. Madeleine cringed to think of the names he had called her the next day. He had looked at her as if he hated her, as if he were afraid of her. *Mon Dieu*, she wondered what she had done that was so unspeakable.

But, when she looked at the results of that night, she knew she regretted nothing. It didn't matter what Jacques thought. Her child was worth her being looked at as if she were a whore. She was worth her having been drugged, for she knew that was what Rima had done. She smiled to herself thinking of how worried Rima was that next day, obviously afraid Madeleine would be angry with her; but, in spite of an incredible headache, Madeleine had acted as if nothing unusual had happened. Neither woman ever talked about it directly, nor did Madeleine ever indicate any resentment. She had even at times with a shy, puzzled smile suggested subtly to Rima that she was glad that it had happened, for she knew the result was what she had wanted so badly—a child of her own.

Madeleine had felt even that night that she had conceived. Rima obviously thought so too. They both started
making clothes for a baby even before there were any
signs that she was *enceinte*. How easy and happy that
pregnancy and birth were! Madeleine had snapped out of
what she called her vapors and regained her vigorous energy, never to lose it again. People had acted as if Madeleine would have a difficult time because she was twenty-
five. She remembered that Sister Pauline had been concerned because she was so muscular, but it was an easy
birth.

Solange was so much prettier than her mother, Madeleine thought, so much easier and relaxed with people. She
was like quicksilver, able to change her mood to suit the
occasion. She did not have her mother's rigid standards.
Madeleine believed that life would be so much easier for
her daughter than it has been for her. Fortunately, Solange
had her father's gaiety and charm. That would smooth the
way for her, that is, if she did not also have her father's
weaknesses. She vowed to be stricter with Solange to balance out Jacques' bad traits.

Madeleine wondered how Solange would give free rein
to the looseness of character that she might have inherited
from her father. Gambling was his main vice, but it was
unlikely Solange would have the opportunity to become a
compulsive gambler. Though most French women liked
their card games privately, there was too much social
pressure on them to leave to their men the glory and despair of the real games of chance like faro and dice. Looking
at her daughter now, Madeleine wondered just how
Jacques's wildness might be reflected in Solange's adult

behavior. Would she inherit his sensuality? And how about her own streak of abandon she displayed the night Solange was conceived? Was that in Solange also, only not so hidden?

"*Maman*," Solange interrupted her thoughts, "why are we going to New Orleans so early this year? It is only October. And why aren't Rima and Mary Claire coming with us?"

"Solange, I never know which question to answer first. We are moving to New Orleans early this year so you can enroll in the Ursulines' school, as I have already explained to you."

"I don't want to be taught by nuns. They wear ugly dresses. They look like big hungry birds ready to swoop down and eat children."

"Solange!" Madeleine warned.

"Besides, I am smart enough already. You can teach me all I need to know. You know more than anybody," Solange said sweetly, but Madeleine knew she was trying to persuade her with compliments. "I want to stay at Magnolia Grove and learn how to grow rice and indigo."

"You don't need to know how to grow rice and indigo. What you need is to learn how to be ladylike and modest. I don't seem to be able to teach you that." Madeleine knew these would be difficult lessons for the child, who was accustomed to running free on the farm with Mary Claire and the Mueller boys. And now that the de Villeres had moved onto the plantation south of them, she had a new playmate. Their youngest son Phillipe was as wild as Solange. Poor Rima could handle one, but not both of them at once. It was time Madeleine took more of an active role in training her daughter. She felt guilty that she had not already set a better example by staying in the house more and teaching her to sew and cook. Thank God she had more field hands now and did not have to work outside so much. And Rima's sons, David and Saul, now ten and eleven, were big enough to help in the fields. Madeleine smiled as she always did when she thought of the boys' Biblical names, chosen, she knew, to please her.

She was glad that Moses had gotten over his resentment about Mary Claire enough to take an interest in the farm again. She felt safe leaving it in his charge, and she knew that Klaus Mueller too would help look after things for her. Now she would be able to stay in town more and set a better example for Solange, who often acted more like a wild boy than a well-behaved girl.

"But, *Maman*," Solange persisted, "you didn't tell me why Rima and Mary Claire aren't coming with us. Will they come later?"

"*Non*, Rima has her own family to take care of, and Mary Claire belongs with her." Yes, she thought, Mary Claire belongs anywhere but in New Orleans where people will see the similarity between her and Solange.

Solange pouted, "But who will cook for us?"

"I will do most of the cooking this winter in New Orleans."

Solange's eyes widened, "You, *Maman*?"

"*Oui*, I am a very good cook. Our life will be a lot different from now on."

"I don't want our life to be different. I like it the way it is. I like you the way you are. You can do things most papas do."

Yes, thought Madeleine, that is the problem.

Then Solange remembered, "Why can't Mary Claire

come with us even if Rima can't? You can be her mama."

"That won't do!" Madeleine snapped. She continued more kindly. "You will find some nice playmates at the Ursulines' school. They will be more suitable for you."

Solange cried indignantly, "I don't want someone suitable! I want Mary Claire! She is fun."

"You think she is fun because she follows you around and does everything you tell her."

"No, I love her. She is like my sister."

Madeleine snapped again. "Don't say that. She is not like your sister. That is impossible. She is a slave; you are her mistress. And you must start thinking of yourself that way."

Solange fought back tears and became quiet, this time keeping her thoughts to herself. *No, never, I will never treat her like a slave. That means I would have to beat her like Monsieur de Villere does his slaves. It is a good thing Phillipe is not like his papa, she thought, or I would not be his friend. I wish I had a tutor like Phillipe and his brothers do, so I could stay at Magnolia Grove. I guess the de Villeres are richer than we are.*

Even as she instructed Solange to treat Mary Claire like a slave, Madeleine felt a guilty ache, for she was looking at the broad back of Lying Boy as he guided the pirogue skillfully and carefully into the outskirts of the city. He too was a slave, however free-spirited; yet in many ways Madeleine regarded him with motherly affection and trusted him completely. Still, like most women of her position, she accepted slavery as the natural order of things; and, if that order were to be kept, a certain decorum was necessary.

"Solange, I do not mean that you cannot still play with Mary Clare, but you must start to think of your social position. We are one of the leading families of New Orleans. We must start to act like one. That includes me as well as you."

Solange was shocked at the idea of her mother ever acting in any way unsuitable. She remained quiet for a while, and Lying Boy took this opportunity to tell a long story about a fight he had had with an alligator while fishing the day before.

Madeleine started to take more of an interest in the passing scene again. The closer they got to New Orleans the more there was to see. There were fewer woods and more houses. The houses seemed to get grander every year, she thought wistfully. Charles Boudreaux had added another wing to Oak Forest, she noticed, and Romain Lafourche had one of those new sheds made of masonry and cement. This must be to store his tobacco. She had watched enviously as his field hands gathered the leaves in big round baskets. She wished she could expand and plant tobacco, but all her acreage was under cultivation. Though Magnolia Grove was an established small plantation, she did not dare grow any larger. Already her success was being talked about and embarrassing Jacques. The talk also embarrassed her, she had to admit; for she was ever fearful that someone would discover she was not a de Mandeville.

She looked curiously at the new industries they were passing: so many new sawmills, indigo factories, silk factories, and brickyards. She wondered if she might secretly invest in one. *Non*, it would be too risky. She knew no one in the businesses that would keep such a secret, even if they agreed to be partners with a woman. Besides, what did she know of factories? She knew only farming. Also, she had to admit to herself that she always needed to keep some extra *livres* in the lining of the *casquette* to keep Jacques's gambling debts down.

As they sighted the pointed steeple of the church of St. Louis, close to the governor's residence, Madeleine turned her neck around and looked as eagerly as Solange. They stepped out onto the *quai* and waited for Lying Boy to secure the pirogue and get their trunks. The wharf was bursting with activity. Solange and Madeleine watched as rice, tobacco, and wine were loaded onto barges. Madeleine noticed how much bigger the warehouse of Maxent, Laclede, and Company had grown. She told Solange that this company had exclusive rights to the fur trade passing through New Orleans from the upper Mississippi. She could hardly pull her daughter's attention away from the boats. Boats were another passion of Solange's. She begged Lying Boy constantly to take her for rides in his pirogue. Once she was caught trying to take it out on the river herself. Madeleine sometimes accused her of having Mississippi river water in her veins instead of blood.

Madeleine exclaimed at how much the town had grown. So many more houses had gone up, and the streets were filled with the four-horse carriages popularized by *Madame* de Pradel, a social leader of New Orleans. The *banquettes*, or sidewalks, were crowded by the new soldiers, lately ordered to New Orleans to build up her defenses. Madeleine now believed what she had heard, that the town had changed a great deal since the new governor, Pierre Regaut, the Marquis de Vaudreuil, and his wife had arrived last year to replace old Governor Bienville. She realized she would have to get accustomed to the town all over again.

Chapter 29

While Lying Boy took their trunks to the Parraults' old house, Madeleine and Solange walked to the new Ursuline convent and hospital on Conde Street between Barracks and Hospital Streets. The sisters had moved there from their temporary quarters at the Bienville Hotel a few years after Madeleine came to New Orleans. The sisters, cheerfully tough in their dealings with the varied people who came to them for spiritual or physical aid, had won wider and wider acceptance among the citizenry, most of whom were at least nominally Catholics. They exerted a civilizing influence on the rowdy frontier town. As a result of their influence, the Ursuline order received direct financial aid from some of the leading figures of the city as well as from the French government. Madeleine looked at their spacious, new fenced-in building and felt a soft glow of pride because of her long association with the Sisters.

As Madeleine and Solange started to enter the gate,

Madeleine had to pull her daughter away from a bullfrog that leaped out of the muddy street onto the sidewalk. "Well, some things never change," Madeleine mumbled. "The streets have not improved."

Sister Pauline greeted them at the door with fluttering excitement. "Madeleine, it has been so long since you visited us. Solange! How you have grown! *Tres jolie!* Oh, you shall never guess who has called on us."

Madeleine sensed his presence even before she looked up and saw him standing so tall by the fireplace. "Captain Beauchamp!" she exclaimed.

"*Bonjour, Madame*, it is good to see you again. And this is your daughter? Sister Pauline is right; she is *tres jolie*, as pretty as her mother." He took Madeleine's hand and brushed his lips over it. She felt the tickle of his beard long after he straightened up and suddenly did not know what to do with her hands, so she put them behind her back.

Solange gave him a perfunctory curtsy and looked curiously at her mother, who was blushing. Madeleine thought how glad she was that she had decided to wear her new green velvet dress. Captain Beauchamp thought how little she had changed, her figure as trim as ever and her face glowing with health. They all sat down a little stiffly. Sister Pauline motioned to Bette to bring them some tea and prattled merrily, seeming to notice nothing amiss. But she, perhaps wiser than her chatter would indicate, was remembering their voyage aboard *les Belles Soeurs*, when she had often glimpsed the captain and Madeleine together. Although their conduct had been perfectly proper, she felt even then that a powerful man-woman attraction was at work between them. Now, years later, after so many of the captain's voyages and so many of

Madeleine's struggles, she still sensed their mutual attraction. She promised herself severe penance for the secret enjoyment she got from watching their nervously proper conduct, their exaggerated formality as they politely made small talk.

"Madeleine, my dear, how nice that you finally meet our captain again. He used to come see us every summer when you were at Magnolia Grove and always asked about you, did you not, Captain Beauchamp? Then he started coming in winter also, but you stopped coming to New Orleans in winter. So here you are at last. Oh, thank you, Bette."

Sister Pauline paused for a breath while she poured them some tea then went on. "Solange, *ma petite*, did you know that the captain brought your mama and me to New Orleans from France on a big ship fifteen years ago? Fifteen years! It hardly seems possible."

Solange looked at the captain with more interest, while balancing the delicate cup on her crossed knee and swinging her foot ever so gently. Her mother gave her a stern look and the foot became still until her mother looked away distractedly; then it swung again ever so slightly.

As the silence began to get awkward, Sister Pauline exclaimed. "Oh, Captain, you must tell Madeleine the news. Madeleine, the captain is about to become your neighbor."

Madeleine was so startled she jumped, which startled Solange so much that her cup tilted and some tea spilled on her dress. She nonchalantly dropped her left hand to cover the stain, uncrossing her knee to aid in balancing the cup.

Madeleine was surprised not just by Sister Pauline's

revelation but also by being forced back to the reality of the present. Just seeing those powerful shoulders bulging in the tight-fitting coat had sent her mind back a decade and a half, away from this sultry land to the pitching deck of *les Belles Soeurs*. She could still feel the hard strength of the man as he had held her tightly, protectively, yet fondly as the angry waves rocked the ship. Despite the years that had passed and her experiences of wife, mother, farmer, and businesswoman, she could still summon up the memory of his clean, salty smell. Reluctantly she let go of the memory and wrenched herself back to the present.

Madeleine asked as calmly as she could, "You have moved close to the Parraults' old house, *Monsieur*?"

Sister Pauline spoke for him, "*Non*, not a neighbor in New Orleans, at Magnolia Grove."

Madeleine found this hard to believe. "You have become a farmer?"

Captain Beauchamp looked uncomfortable. "Uh, no, I just decided to invest in some land near New Orleans. I will probably sell it when it goes up in value."

"He bought your and Jacques's old land, Madeleine, the twenty acres that you lost to the Company."

Madeleine turned to him again in surprise. He tried to explain, "Yes, when I heard your land was up for sale by the Company, it seemed the perfect opportunity to, uh, make an investment."

"Then you do not intend to build on the land?" Madeleine asked, trying to hide her relief.

Captain Beauchamp rushed to reassure her, "Oh, no. It is merely an investment. I have begun to spend a little more time on land, but I prefer to be in the city."

Captain Beauchamp marveled at Madeleine's beauty

and dignity, just as he had when he first saw her aboard ship when she was a *casquette* girl bound for the unsettled colony in New Orleans. In the years since, there had been many voyages, many women of fleeting pleasure; but Madeleine, more than any other, kept alive the fires of interest in a home and family ashore. Yes, he thought wryly to himself, I want to be in a city, all right, but the right city for me would be one with Madeleine in it! She is indeed a better de Mandeville than the de Mandevilles themselves. If only I had not been such a fool as to let her marry someone else—especially that womanizing Jacques Bouligny, he thought bitterly.

"Will you be staying in New Orleans for a while?" Madeleine asked politely, telling herself to breathe naturally while waiting for the answer.

"*Oui*, for at least a month while my ship is being repaired. One of your pesky bars on the Mississippi damaged my hull."

Madeleine smiled, "Is it *les Belles Soeurs* that is being repaired?"

Captain Beauchamp looked straight into her eyes. "*Non*, it is one of my other ships. I have three now, but my favorite is still *les Belle Soeurs*. It holds fond memories for me."

Solange noticed that her mother blushed for the second time. What a curious effect this man has on her, she thought. Even at seven years old, Solange had become a student of human nature, especially of adults, who, she thought, seemed to act their parts more deliberately than children do. Mary Claire might play a fool or a drunken Indian or a scolding mother, but that was always done in fun, an obvious bit of make believe. With adults, you never could tell for sure; they seemed to have a different manner for each person they met. Her mother right now, for example, did not seem the bossy, serious woman that she appeared to be most of the time. Solange looked slyly over at her mother and noted that she seemed somehow younger all of a sudden and certainly more subdued. This man must have meant something to her at one time, she thought, maybe before I came into the world. But I wonder why she seems so quiet and uncertain. He is handsome in a rough sort of way, but not handsomer than *Papa*. The thought startled her. Surely *Maman* does not like this man better than *Papa*!

Solange shook her skirt a little, trying to dry it. The motion of the skirt caused her to spill some tea on the right side. She darted a look at her mother and could not believe her good fortune. She was looking at the tall man instead of at Solange.

The captain broke this second long silence to take his leave. He graciously expressed his thanks to Sister Pauline and complimented Madeleine and Solange again politely, telling them he hoped to see them again. The room seemed very empty to Madeleine after he left. Sister Pauline rescued Solange from the untamable cup by sending her outside to look at the grounds. Solange turned her back on her mother as quickly as possible to prevent her seeing the wet dress. She need not have bothered; Madeleine was oblivious to her.

"Now, my dear, we must have a nice chat. Have you seen Jacques yet?" Sister Pauline asked with a rare serious tone in her voice.

"*Non*, we came straight here from the Parraults' old house."

"When are you going to stop calling it the Parraults' house? Haven't you told anyone yet that it is now your house?"

Madeleine answered worriedly, "Only you and the Parraults know that I bought their house when they moved to a larger one because of their growing brood. I told Jacques that we were renting it. He would be furious if he knew I made such a large transaction without consulting him, and I could not let him know I had that much money."

"But he must know you are paying his gambling debts."

Madeleine answered sadly, "I think he pretends not to know, for I never give the money directly to him. If he admitted to himself that I was paying them, he would have to forbid me to do it. Then he would have stop gambling. I make it as easy as possible for him to maintain his dignity. I send Lying Boy to his creditors and tell him to say the money is from Jacques."

"Do you think anybody believes him, Madeleine?"

"Perhaps they too pretend to themselves. I think they would rather think they were taking the money from Jacques than from me." The two women sat in a companionable silence now.

As she listened to her own statement, Madeleine could not help wondering about the etiquette of gambling in general, not just in the games themselves but in the payment of debts, as in Jacques's case. Some men try to keep up the façade of honor, no matter how despicable their behavior.

Sister Pauline hesitated and then said, "Jacques is greatly altered, you know. You must prepare yourself and Solange for seeing him."

"How do you mean *altered*? Do you mean from his drinking or has he been ill?" Madeleine could not imagine Jacques looking anything but handsome and immaculate.

Sister Pauline answered her evasively, "Perhaps a little of both. Now, let us find Solange and show her around the school."

Chapter 30

Jacques was waiting in the darkened parlor of the Parraults' old home when Madeleine and Solange arrived. Solange ran to him with outstretched arms and cried out eagerly, "*Papa, Papa!* I hoped you would be here."

Jacques picked her up and swung her around, then quickly put her down because he was out of breath. Madeleine pulled the drapes to let some light in the room just as Jacques turned to face her. She gasped as she got a good look at him. It was not just the specifics of appearance that disturbed her but rather his general manner. Whether moving or at rest, he seemed old, terribly old, as if his joints were solidifying, thus making it difficult to bend or even to stand or sit. Although he tried to romp with his daughter as he had before, Madeleine could see the slowness and the exertion it took even in the simplest of movements—holding up a picture for the child to see, poking a forefinger into her tummy to produce a giggle, patting her bottom as she ran by. Madeleine felt much of her displeasure with him melt in compassion.

"Hello, Madeleine," Jacques greeted his wife, "you haven't told me how well I am looking. You are looking lovely, as always. Isn't that a new dress?"

Madeleine tried to be diplomatic. "It is good to see you, Jacques. I am surprised to see that you are *not* looking well. Have you been sick?"

Jacques avoided her question. "Such wifely concern touches me." He turned back to Solange, pulled her onto his knee, and started asking her questions about her summer. Madeleine took this opportunity to study him. She could hardly believe how he had changed in the two years since she had seen him. His complexion was yellow and dry, his face cadaverous, with dark, drooping circles under his eyes. His body too was gaunt, but for the first time he had a paunch. Madeleine noticed, however, that he was still well groomed in a clean, pressed uniform and polished boots. He was wearing a cologne that did not quite hide the sick odor that emanated from him.

Solange did not seem to notice anything different about her father. She obviously adored him, even though she rarely saw him. In Madeleine's opinion, she adored him *because* she rarely saw him. He used every bit of charm and wit he possessed with his daughter, and she responded in kind. He brought her frivolous gifts and laughed and sang with her as her mother never did. Madeleine was the disciplinarian with Solange; Jacques was the playmate and suitor. Madeleine taught her and took care of her when she was ill; Jacques enjoyed her when she was well.

Madeleine left them now to walk through her house

and feel the pride of possession. She opened windows and dusted a piece of furniture here and there. As she was putting away her clothes in what had been the Parraults' sunlit, spacious bedroom, Jacques came in and sat on the bed. Madeleine looked up but continued her task. "Where is Solange?"

"She is in the back yard playing with her new dog."

Madeleine raised an eyebrow but said nothing. Jacques said, "When Lying Boy said you were coming here, I took the liberty of bringing my clothes over from the barracks and putting them in our old room in the back. I trust you have no objection to your husband living in the same house with you?"

The remark was bitter, of course, but Madeleine thought she detected a slight whine of self-pity, something she had never noticed in him before. "It is you who have stayed away, Jacques."

Although she still felt some slight guilt about her abandoned performance on the night of Solange's conception, she had come to feel in recent years that his disdain for her had become tiresome, almost ridiculous. Sometimes she suspected that he had rejected her not because he could not countenance such sensuality but because he wanted an excuse not to come to her bed. And why was that? Other women? Of course. She knew that Jacques before and certainly after their marriage took his pleasure with other women, usually trollops in the gambling dens or even, she suspected, with some of the low-life camp followers. She wondered if he had resumed his affair with Marie, if that was why he went to O'Brien's Pub so often. But were there other reasons? Had he become impotent? As she looked at him with all the objectivity she could muster, she felt that right now this broken man was not interested in any carnal pleasures at all.

She finally answered his question. "No objections at all. I am glad to have you here. It will be good for Solange to get to know you better." Madeleine, even though she realized that her comment could be interpreted as sarcastic, was entirely sincere. Any child, especially a beautiful vivacious little girl like Solange, needed masculinity as a counterbalance to a life spent with mostly women. After all, Jacques had passed on a part of himself to the girl, and perhaps Solange could profit from the dual mirror images of both father and mother. Somehow, on some level, Madeleine realized that, whatever association could be built up between the two, it would be brief; for, though she did not say the word and tried not to even think it, death seemed to hang on him like an invisible mantle.

Jacques looked at her suspiciously to see if she were being sarcastic. "Solange tells me you saw your old beau at the convent. Is that why you go there so often? To meet him?"

"Jacques, I have been in New Orleans only three or four times in the last eight years. And, if you mean Captain Beauchamp, this was the first time I have seen him in the fifteen years since I first arrived in Louisiana." It always surprised Madeleine when Jacques had these occasional outbursts of jealousy. Once he insisted she was Klaus's mistress and that he was the reason she stayed at Magnolia Grove so much. A few times she caught him even watching how she acted with Lying Boy. The outbursts had started right after that strange night when Solange was conceived.

Jacques snarled at her, "Then tell me, *ma cherie*, why

did your Captain Beauchamp buy the land next to yours? Perhaps as a wedding present for you when I am dead?"

"What do you mean by *when you are dead*? Are you ill? Tell me what is wrong with you." Madeleine became concerned for him.

"Nothing is wrong with me but hard living. The drink, rich food, and late nights have finally taken their toll, just as you always said they would. But, my sober wife, I would rather go out in a frenzy of parties than live forever as you do in that self-disciplined, careful life of yours."

"Perhaps I do not live entirely as I wish."

Jacques looked at her speculatively. "*Non*, perhaps you do not. We both know you are capable of great passion, but not for me, that is, not unless you have been drugged."

Madeleine tried to make peace with him. "I do not know what was wrong with me that night. I have never felt that way before or since. I barely remember what happened. I must have acted dreadful for you never to come to my bed again."

Jacques turned his head from her to look out the window at Solange. "Not so dreadful. It's just that it did not seem like you, but at least we got Solange from that night." He remembered that night well, perhaps too well, he sometimes thought. Her behavior was such a contrast to what he had seen in her up to that time—from her shocked frigidity on their wedding night to her calm but non-participating acceptance in the months and years that followed, years during which he often tumbled a lively-skilled whore just to get the feeling, however false, that some woman wanted him. That night at Magnolia Grove had shaken the view he had always had of his wife. The depth and abandon of her passion that night had frightened him away for a while. Then, when he might have returned to her bed, he discovered—but, no, he must not think of that....

Madeleine sat beside him on the bed and put her hand gently on his arm. "Jacques, Solange and I will stay in New Orleans more from now on. Moses can oversee Magnolia Grove with very little supervision. Is it too late for us to live as husband and wife again?"

Jacques pulled his arm away as if it had been burned. He got up and paced. "It *is* too late. Can't you see that?"

Madeleine saw only that he still did not want her. Was she so unattractive then? Or was he still thinking of her unspeakable behavior that night? Perhaps he was really ill. She decided to ask Anne Parrault if she knew what was wrong with Jacques. In the meantime, she would change the subject. She resumed putting away her things and re-marked casually, "I was surprised to see so many new officers just walking around town when I arrived. Are we expecting an Indian attack on New Orleans?"

Jacques took a few minutes to compose himself before answering. He sat down again, lit his pipe slowly and care-fully, and took a couple of draws. "No, no expectation of attack. It is just that we are finally over-defended. Louisiana now has thirty-seven military companies. Since Governor Vaudreuil took Bienville's place, discipline has become lax to non-existent. We have a lot of free time. I haven't mounted guard once in fifty days."

They were now able to look at each other for a brief time. Madeleine kept the conversation going. "With so many soldiers in town, at least there must be fewer crimes."

Jacques seemed to warm to his subject now.

"Unfortunately, that is not true. When the Western Company gave up its charter and the governing of Louisiana was returned to the king, the criminal element relocated. When the Company withdrew, most of the criminals came to New Orleans. They were used to a city. After all, a city is the best place to ply their trade—theft and extortion."

Although theft and extortion were indeed rampant in New Orleans during this time, these were not the crimes that kept people at home after dark or forced them to travel in armed groups when that was possible. Robbery, rape, assault, and murder were common crimes, so common that only victims and the victims' survivors seemed to care, for an organized police force was still far in the future. A body tossed into the Mississippi appeared weeks later as an unidentifiable skeleton on a beach bordering the Gulf of Mexico. A woman, gang-raped by the seedy crew of a transient ship, often could not identify her attackers and could get little justice even if she dared admit her disgrace publicly. A businessman going home after a profitable day, his bag loaded with the day's receipts, needed a stout carriage and adequate bodyguards if he hoped to survive. Jacques thought of these unceasing acts of sordid violence that were so much a counterbalance to the city's charm but did not mention them to Madeleine. There was no point, he felt, in him causing her undue concern, for she would certainly learn these frightening truths soon enough.

Madeleine wondered if she had done the best thing to bring Solange to New Orleans. "But, Jacques, surely the soldiers can keep them in line."

Jacques laughed without mirth. "Most of the soldiers are dregs themselves. They are the worst of the royal army. They go around at night stealing chickens and whiskey themselves."

"Yes, I seem to remember Klaus Mueller telling me an awful story about some soldiers escorting guests and produce of his from La Balize to New Orleans. The soldiers made them disembark in front of the cemetery instead of taking them to the Parade Ground as they were supposed to. The soldiers told them they looked like corpses anyway."

Jacques smiled a little. "I was in the barracks when this incident was reported to their officers. They merely laughed. They think the Germans are nothing but country buffoons anyway." His smile indicated to Madeleine that he shared his fellow officers' opinions.

"It is those country buffoons that feed most of the army," Madeleine commented tartly.

"You don't have to defend your German farmers to me, Madeleine. I know their worth."

Madeleine decided it would be safer to divert the conversation from this topic also. "Why doesn't Governor de Vaudreuil stop this kind of behavior? I hear he is an aristocratic gentleman. He surely cannot condone such conduct."

Jacques shook his head sadly. "I am afraid he is corrupt himself. It is in his best interests personally to look the other way at corruption of others. I understand he gets a profit from the numerous alehouses in New Orleans now. His wife, the Marquise de Vaudreuil, forces the merchants to sell potions made by her servant."

Madeleine was shocked. "What kind of potions?"

"Powdered crayfish eyes, stags' horns, and snakeskin are some of the less harmful remedies. I am told that, when her servant is not in, she prepares them herself."

Jacques did not tell Madeleine, but he knew a great deal about drugs in New Orleans. Some, of course, were mere placebos, effective only in the mind of the user. The most prominent of these were the numerous aphrodisiacs sold, with all sorts of startling guarantees, in the bordellos for private use even among some of the most distinguished citizens. Less harmless, he knew from experience, were those that could for a while make one see the world as he would like it to be rather than how it actually is— mysterious seeds from the islands to the south that could be chewed to produce a euphoria much as alcohol can. There was a weed that was often mixed with tobacco and smoked in a small clay pipe. And, of course, there was straight opium, which had become common in sleazy gambling dens near the docks. No, thought Jacques, the Marquise de Vaudreuil and her servant are not the great contributors, just small tributaries in the expanding drug world.

Madeleine shuddered. "You sound as if you disapprove of them, the de Vaudreuils; yet I have heard they entertain lavishly and encourage gaiety. I should think you would enjoy them." She tried not to sound sarcastic but did not quite succeed.

Jacques became downcast. "I do not indulge in society much anymore. You will be relieved to know that you won't be pressured into going to lots of parties during your stay here."

Madeleine found it hard to believe that Jacques had given up parties and cheerful company. Once more a word, unexpressed, not even consciously felt, tingled in Madeleine's consciousness: *death*. If Jacques had really decided not to trot off to every party in a partying city, that was indeed a refreshing change. Though she had often tired of the false conviviality at the many functions she had attended with Jacques in the past, she now felt a twinge of sadness. A man who is well, a man who still has some use for life does not change his habits so drastically. As she glanced up at him, she noticed that he was staring down at the floor and blinking hard, his breathing rather labored. She realized that he no longer had the energy for the boisterous socializing that had once been such an important part of his life.

Chapter 31

Madeleine found that Jacques was true to his word this time. He did not press her to attend any parties, nor did he attend any without her as far as she knew. He went out almost every night, came home late, slept till noon, then got up and played with their daughter, Solange, when she came home from the Ursuline School for Girls. He had dinner with them every evening and was unfailingly polite to Madeleine. At times they appeared to be a normal family. At least both Madeleine and Jacques hoped that their family life seemed normal, especially to Solange. Despite their failures as husband and wife, they wanted only the best for their lone offspring, who showed such promise of growing into a woman of exceptional beauty and intelligence.

In the hours after Solange's school and before her bedtime, Madeleine and Jacques played their roles conscientiously—he the indulgent and concerned father, she the good mother and housewife. Apparently their acting

235

worked and became for each of them more of a pleasure than a duty as they saw the product of their mating blossoming into such a charming girl, for Solange seemed to become warmer, more content with life in the city. She worked hard in school and eagerly shared with her parents the successes and failures of the day. She expressed her love more openly toward her father, giving him little hugs and kisses, which he eagerly reciprocated. She even warmed toward her mother, occasionally putting an unexpected peck on Madeleine's cheek or helping her to prepare and serve the intimate dinner for three that became a cozy but guarded routine for all of them.

Madeleine assumed that Jacques was going to O'Brien's Pub, his favorite haunt, on the nights he went out, until she asked him one night as he was leaving about Marie and Michael. He snapped at her that he had not seen them in a year and never intended to see them again.

Madeleine was puzzled but his attitude did not allow for any more questions. She resumed her volunteer work at the Ursulines' school, orphanage, and hospital. It was as if she had never been away. Word got around that the *casquette* angel of mercy was back. This time, to Madeleine's surprise, Jacques did not object to her activities outside the home. He acted as if he had lost the right to question her movements. Sometimes she almost missed his old possessiveness.

It was obvious to Madeleine that Jacques was getting sicker and weaker each day. Sometimes Madeleine heard him moaning in his sleep. Frequently she was awakened by the sound of his pacing in his room. She knew he was drinking more, but it was a steady, controlled drinking rather than the binges he used to go on. She wondered if he were drinking now to kill pain that he would not admit to having.

Madeleine worried about Jacques's health, yet she knew of nothing that she could do. Certainly, if he could be helped by medical attention, he would have taken the necessary steps to get help. She suspected that he had some incurable ailment, perhaps even a congenital one, and that Jacques, well aware of his fate, was calling upon all his soldierly courage to bear up bravely. And brave he was indeed, she felt, for often she could see the pain ripple through him, even though he had developed a tight-faced, almost stoic manner. Though he drank almost constantly, he never seemed to lack control of himself. Madeleine guessed that his unsteadiness was the result of his illness more than mere drunkenness. More and more he seemed to Madeleine like a plant that was being cut off from water or some other important nutrient. He was slowly wilting, unalterably but proudly, as if he sought to salvage honor from the indignity of his condition by focusing his thoughts not on what he was at that time but on what he had been.

Whenever Madeleine questioned Anne Parrault about what was wrong with Jacques, she was evasive. Finally, one day, instead of answering, Anne asked Madeleine a strange question, one that embarrassed them both.

"Madeleine, my dear, I must ask you this for your own good. Do you and Jacques sleep in the same bed?"

Madeleine almost did not answer but then said cautiously, "*Non*, we have separate rooms. May I ask what this has to do with his being ill?"

Anne persisted, "But do you visit each other during the night; that is, do you, I mean to say...?"

Madeleine replied sharply to her old friend, "I know what you mean to say. I don't wonder that you have trouble saying it."

"*Mon Dieu*, Madeleine," Anne said with some exasperation, "you can be a stiff-necked prude. Sometimes it is hard to believe that you ever lived in Paris."

Madeleine finally began to see what she was hinting at, and she paled at the thought. "Oh, no, are you suggesting that Jacques has a disease of the, I mean, a sexually related illness?" It was her turn to stumble over her words.

"Oh, my dear, I did not want to tell you. Robert told me finally when I kept asking Jacques over and over again to see a doctor. Robert told me that he got his illness at the rooms over O'Brien's Pub. He suspects that either Marie or Michael arranged for Jacques to be with a prostitute that they knew to be diseased. He believes Jacques suspects the same, but he refuses to discuss it with Robert."

Madeleine knew from her studies with the Ursuline nuns and her work at Charity Hospital that Jacques must be in the last stages of his sickness and would soon die in agony. Already he was talking about moving back to the barracks. He obviously wanted to spare Solange the sight of him dying. To think that Marie might be responsible! She remembered Marie's unreasonable rage at her that day she and the other *casquette* girls arrived in New Orleans and knew Jacques's former mistress was capable of getting revenge. Maybe Marie had hoped he would pass the disease on his wife.

Anne's revelation jolted Madeleine into a confused turbulence of thought. At first she thought how stupid she had been not to recognize the nature of Jacques's ailment;

after all, she had seen others in the hospital afflicted in a similar fashion. Then, when she wondered about the time of the onset of the dread ailment, she could not help speculating if that was why he shunned her bed all these years. Did he really not want me? Or was he afraid of infecting me too? That thought, however fleeting, filled her with a flood of compassion for this broken, dying man.

After a long silence with Madeleine simply sitting and Anne looking at her worriedly, Madeleine got up abruptly. "I must go now. Thank you, Anne, for telling me finally. Perhaps I can help him now that I know what I am dealing with. At least I can be more understanding." The two friends embraced and Madeleine left, her legs trembling as she walked away.

Life in the Bouligny household slowly began to change. Madeleine became much kinder to Jacques and did what she could to make him more comfortable. She saw to it that Solange did not tire him. Sometimes he looked at Madeleine as if he knew why she had become so solicitous of his health, but he said nothing. He took a leave from the army and asked Madeleine to pack away most of his uniforms. They both knew he would never wear them again. Finally, he stopped going out at night and withdrew to his room. Though he was visibly weaker and sicker, he remained scrupulously clean and well groomed. Every night, he dressed and joined Solange and Madeleine at dinner.

Madeleine knew he was in extreme pain whenever he was unable to make the effort to talk. When this happened she filled in the gaps for him and uncharacteristically chattered about anything that came to her mind. She filled him in on her last few years at Magnolia Grove and told him about her dreams of it someday becoming a large working plantation. She described in detail what he had missed in Solange's growing up, from her first step to her learning to ride and shoot from Lying Boy and her love of the river. She even repeated some of Lying Boy's more colorful stories until Jacques shook with laughter and begged her to stop.

Solange joined her mother in recounting some of the years at Magnolia Grove, delighting Jacques when she elaborated on some narrative of Madeleine's. With her mother's help at times, she would recall childhood experiences that her father would have never known about; and he, despite his weakened condition, would insist on prolonging the sessions. He had a ravenous curiosity about anything that had affected Solange's early years. Although she was not aware, as her mother was, of Jacques's true illness, Solange was not blind. She could tell by her father's appearance, which was worsening daily, and by her mother's increased solicitude that these mutually rewarding feasts of reminiscence would not go on much longer. She talked more now, especially when her words seemed to give her father pleasure, but without prompting she slackened the exuberance and duration of her physical play with Jacques. Instead of sneaking up and tickling him as she used to do, she would playfully quiz him about something she had learned that day in school. Thus, the quiet evenings became preciously important for all of them, though perhaps for different reasons. Solange felt an invigorating pride in being part of a complete family.

When Solange was not in the room, in a halting voice, Madeleine would tell him about her own childhood as a peasant then as a servant on the de Mandeville estate. It seemed to her that he no longer looked at her with distaste, but with compassion when she talked of this. There were times when he doubled over with pain, but he did not cry out. She would look away and pretend not to notice.

Madeleine reduced her volunteer work at Charity Hospital to a few hours a week, when she was most needed. Late on the afternoon of New Year's Eve, she was preparing to leave for the hospital to help dress the wounds of some people whose barge had been attacked by renegade Chickasaw Indians. Jacques came out of his room dressed to go out. He was walking with a cane, but walking erect, and dressed impeccably.

Although Jacques wore civilian clothing, an objective observer would have detected much of the military in his bearing—this in spite of the obviously painful slowness of his movements. He stood tall and straight, his shoulders held back into the tailored perfection of his jacket. His boots were brilliantly shined, emphasizing the sharp, deliberate steps, however slow. Although he seemed slightly ashamed of the cane, it added a note of authority to his commanding presence.

Madeleine was alarmed to see him going out. She knew it must have taken a superhuman effort because his mouth was tight with pain. But a look from him warned her not to object. She said evenly, "Have a nice evening, Jacques. Be sure to take your overcoat. It is cold out." She waited for him to help her with her own cape. He leaned his cane carefully against a chair and with a gesture of gentle affection snuggled the cape about her shoulders, giving her a pat on each upper arm when he had finished. He then opened the door and ushered her out with a slight bow. They walked off in opposite directions, she in the direction of Charity Hospital and he toward the tavern district on Exchange Street.

Chapter 32

Madeleine administered to the sick and wounded that afternoon and into the evening strictly by rote. She did her work well, as she always did, but her thoughts were on her husband Jacques. Time after time she recreated in her mind their final minutes together at the house, trying to recall some clue in his behavior. Why had he decided to go out after so many evenings at home? Was it just the holiday atmosphere? Considering his general mood of late, when he was content merely to rest until he spent time with his wife and daughter at the end of the day, she did not think it likely that he would rouse himself with such great effort just to help bring in the year 1743. No, she felt, there must be some other motive. Was there any clue in his dress? Not really, she thought, because he has always dressed well, fashionably but not gaudily. Madeleine mentally slapped herself and tried to pay even closer attention to the wounded man who had been temporarily placed in the hallway; but, even as she tended him, her thoughts went back again to Jacques. She wondered, with a slight touch of panic and guilt, whether she would ever see him again.

Besides the barge victims, the hospital was filled with the usual New Year's Eve revelers with knife and gunshot wounds. Some were merely drunk and half frozen from passing out on the street. One man was brought in soaking wet. He had left a bar and decided to take a swim, so he dove off the levee into the ice-cold Mississippi River. His hair and eyebrows were stiff with ice. Madeleine went through the motions of helping people but her mind remained on Jacques. She wished Lying Boy were in New Orleans so he could go look for him. But it would have been too awkward to have Lame Doe in the same house. She knew she did not dare ask anyone else; Jacque would be furious. The sisters looked at her with sympathy and gave her little pats as they passed her in the halls, but they dared not ask the proud Madeleine Bouligny what troubled her.

Just as Madeleine was preparing to leave at midnight, another man covered with blood was brought in. Sister Pauline took one look at him and asked Madeleine to wait in her office. When Madeleine saw that Robert Parrault was one of the men who had brought him in, she stifled a scream. Knowing what she would see, she shook off Sister Pauline, walked over to the table, and looked down at Jacques's pale, still face. She forced herself to ask, "Is he dead?"

Sister Pauline said kindly, "No, not quite, but he has obviously lost a lot of blood, and he seems to have been stabbed near the heart. He does not have much stamina.

You must prepare yourself, my dear. Now, go into my office while we dress his wounds."

"No! I will take care of him. He is my husband."

Robert Parrault pulled her aside and insisted, "Please, Madeleine, your hands are shaking. He is better off in the Sisters' care. We will stand nearby in case he becomes conscious."

Madeleine turned to him and demanded angrily. "What happened to him? Who stabbed him?"

Robert answered reluctantly, "It was Michael O'Brien."

Madeleine said bitterly, "I knew it. Are you sure it was Michael and not Marie? Has he been arrested?"

"No."

"No? Why not? Is he dead?" Robert shook his head from side to side and would not look at her. "He is not dead! Then why haven't you arrested him? You are a soldier and Jacques's friend. Will you let him go free?"

"Madeleine, I cannot. It was a fair fight."

He pulled her farther away from the nuns working over Jacques as she hissed furiously, "How can it have been a fair fight? Anybody can see that he was dying. He could barely stand."

"Madeleine, I don't know how to tell you this. I hope you can understand. It was a duel. Jacques's challenged Michael O'Brien to a duel."

Madeleine laughed aloud at this. "A duel? My Jacques challenged a pub owner, husband of a prostitute, to a *duel*? A duel of knives when he is an expert with the sword and a gun?"

"He had to give O'Brien the choice of weapons since he made the challenge."

Madeleine tried to comprehend what he was saying,

but it made no sense. "Why did Jacques challenge such a man? He is coarse and common. Besides he had not gone near O'Brien's Pub since.... Was it because of...?"

Robert knew what she was trying to say. "It may have been partly because of that."

"But why would he have waited so long? Why would he wait until he was so weak to challenge him?"

Robert would not answer her. Madeleine grabbed the large, kindly man's lapels and shook him. "I have a right to know. Tell me, blast you!"

The Sisters looked up from their administrations over Jacques in shock at Madeleine. She insisted more quietly, "Tell me, Robert."

Robert finally said with resignation, "Only Jacques knows for certain, Madeleine. I was told that Jacques came into O'Brien's Pub looking for Michael. They got into an argument, but not over the cause of his sickness. That was not mentioned."

"Then what in the name of all that is holy did they argue about, the weather? Don't look away from me. Tell me!"

Robert lost his temper. "Do you never let up, Madeleine? They argued about you."

Madeleine was completely taken aback. "Me? How could they possibly argue about me? I hardly know the O'Briens. Michael was the clerk on *les Belles Soeurs*, but I rarely saw him after he checked in the *casquette* girls the day we left France."

Robert was uncomfortable. "He evidently mentioned that. He said something about seeing the ship's ledger and your not being a de Mandeville. Evidently Jacques had heard the rumor before, traced it to O'Brien, and challenged him to a duel."

Madeleine could not speak for a moment. So the truth was out at last. It didn't seem to matter now what her name was. Poor, sick Jacques died defending a false name that was unimportant. Madeleine felt a deep shame that he saw how much she valued that name and fought to protect her feelings and reputation.

With some sobering self-criticism, Madeleine recalled a line from one of Shakespeare's plays she had read in the Ursulines' library: "What's in a name? A rose by any other name would smell as sweet...." Yet to her the name de Mandeville had indeed smelled sweeter, and she had spent many years trying to prove it. But now, what did it matter, really? Would her life of the last fifteen years have been different if she had used her real name? Would Jacques have refused to marry her if he had known she was a servant in the de Mandeville estate? Would he still be alive?

Biting her lips into a harsh tightness, she squared her shoulders and turned back to Robert. "So Jacques was stabbed in a knife brawl in a pub over me."

Robert was quick to reassure her. "No, no. It wasn't like that. I told you, Jacques formally challenged him to a duel. He gave O'Brien his choice of weapons, and they both got seconds." He hesitated a moment.

Madeleine said flatly, "You were Jacques's second. You allowed him to kill himself. He could not have defended himself against a sick child. Where did you have this duel," she asked sarcastically, "the Dueling Oak?"

Robert nodded in guilty agreement with all her statements.

"*Mon Dieu*, what fools you men are to cooperate in such a farce, such a dangerous farce." Robert was spared any further comment by Sister Pauline, who called urgently,

"Madeleine, come quickly. He is conscious."

Madeleine rushed to her husband's side, and the Sisters left them alone. Sister Pauline signaled that he did not have much time. Jacques was gasping for breath. "Madeleine?"

"Yes, Jacques, I am here." She took his hand and tried to warm it with her own. "Jacques, why did you do this? The de Mandeville name was not worth dying for. Besides, I have yours now. It is enough."

"*Non*, let us be honest finally. It was never enough. You must not feel guilty. It was not just for you that I challenged him. I would have used any excuse. Is it not better that I die this way than the other? It is more fitting."

The tears started to flow down Madeleine's cheeks at the idea of Jacques staging his own suicide. How like him to try to give a common brawl the dignity of a formal duel. Even in her grief, which came as a jolting climax of finality to a decade and a half of a most unconventional married relationship, Madeleine could not keep her thoughts from turning again to a concept that she had entertained scornfully before. Where was honor in all this? Earlier she had thought of the male ego in connection with gambling and with cuckoldry, in both of which much importance was attached to honor, to the public face that showed to the world, regardless of what ugliness and untruth lurked behind. But now, thinking of poor, weak Jacques engaging in a duel he could not hope to win—and all in defense of her name, her *honor*—Madeleine was touched with a glint of understanding. Madeleine thought of her own honor, epitomized in the name de Mandeville, and she wept as

Jacques breathed his last breath.

Chapter 33

In the weeks and months and years following Jacques's death, the relationship between Madeleine and her daughter became not exactly closer, but interdependent in ways that neither of them could define. Solange, certainly an individual in her own right and determined to stay that way, was like a chameleon in adapting to city life. She affected a minimum of good manners and ladylike deportment most of the time while in New Orleans. Then, on their increasingly briefer visits to Magnolia Grove, she resumed her uninhibited hoyden ways.

In the city, Solange took on a more ladylike polish, much to Madeleine's satisfaction, as the nuns guided her academically and to a certain extent socially—improving her use of language, making her aware of her French heritage, forcing her to control her volatile temper. Above all, they quietly emphasized the benefits of living her life according to the tenets of Catholicism.

Madeleine found her life too focused in many ways by the influence of the Ursulines. She continued her own nursing work in their hospital and orphanage, as their school guarded and guided her daughter during most of those same hours. Madeleine attended mass daily, usually with Solange, who occasionally protested that a double dose at church and again at school was unfair.

Madeleine attended some of the better social functions in the city. Her attendance was sought after by hosts and hostesses who respected her restraint and formality, if nothing else as a contrast to the typical Gallic gaiety. Her attendance seemed to many a guarantee that the party was important and that influential people were getting together to celebrate the city's growing status as a center of industry and trade, the city that made the great river a functioning tool for commerce.

Madeleine, still comparatively young and strikingly attractive, was in command of herself and proper in every way. She sometimes seemed to be more a retired matron rather than a marriageable widow. The only man who even attempted to court the aloof *Madame* Bouligny was the occasional visitor to New Orleans, Captain Jean Paul Beauchamp, who escorted her to a few social activities. As far as anyone could determine, he made no progress beyond that of an infrequent escort.

Madeleine thought often of Jean Paul Beauchamp and his proposal of marriage to her two years after Jacques had died. He had started his proposal with an apology.

"Madeleine, I will regret for the rest of my life not asking for your hand onboard *les Belles Soeurs*. I knew before we arrived in New Orleans that I loved you."

"So why didn't you? I would have gladly accepted then."

"Oh, *ma cherie*, it was guilt, guilt and fear that stopped me. I was haunted then by my pregnant wife walking into the ocean and drowning herself because she couldn't bear to be alone for months while I was at sea."

Madeleine tried to comfort him. "That is understandable, Jean Paul. And I knew you had to be at sea most of the time or you would not be happy."

"No, Madeleine, I was a fool not to see then that you were too strong a woman to walk into the sea no matter what I did or didn't do. I could have saved you from Jacques and from your having to work so hard to survive. And I could have saved me from almost two decades of missing you. Marry me now, and we will never be lonely again."

Madeleine was tempted but said, "*Non, mon cher*, I have worked too hard to be independent and will not give that up. Besides, I know you still want to be at sea most of the year."

He did not deny that.

Sometimes she regretted that she had refused him. She still felt a pull toward him whenever he was in the same room, and she missed him when he was at sea. Sometimes when they were at a friend's house playing cards, she looked down at his strong hands and wished he would put them on hers. Whenever he returned from a voyage still smelling of the sea, her senses were reminded of the two times on the ship he took her in his arms. She wished she could be like Suzanne Chauvin and flirt with him, or even like Solange and draw him to her with her warmth. But she could remain only cold and distant, as was her habit. Captain Beauchamp respected that distance and made no more overtures for almost a decade.

According to tradition, a retired sea captain forsakes his ship, goes ashore, perhaps raises a few chickens, smokes his pipe, and lives with his memories. But Captain Beauchamp, though partially retired by the early 1750s, only partially complied with those expectations.

Having seen Louisiana, especially New Orleans, grow from a barely habitable shore base to a thriving agricultural and shipping center, he felt an obligation to help further that growth. He used his vast knowledge of ships and shipping to facilitate movement of people and cargo into and out of the fast-expanding port of New Orleans. Whatever the administration, the Company's or the monarchy's, he had been sought after and consulted on all sorts of maritime matters—the best types of ships for the rivers and for the open seas, the methods of control in docking and unloading craft from all over, and physical improvements that could be made for shore facilities. Although he was not officially in business as a shipping agent, he often functioned as such, mainly because of his skill and experience and his broad range of acquaintances and acceptance among ship captains and ship owners all over the world. Without the quiet guidance and competence of Captain Beauchamp, the development of New Orleans as a major transit area between the Mississippi Valley, with all its wealth, and the Caribbean, South America, and Europe itself would not have taken place with such efficient rapidity.

Always properly attired, he was well respected in the city, a dignified figure as he strolled down the sidewalks, military in his bearing but with the slight roll of the sailor in his walk. Socially, Captain Beauchamp was a number-one consideration for any hostess of the French upper class; so he attended many balls, parties, and other functions, occasionally in the company of Madeleine, whose severe yet pleasant decorum complemented his own. They were a charming couple, so well acquainted after their many years of friendship that some of their mannerisms—the quick, one-pump handshake, the stiff-backed bow of acknowledgment—were almost mirror images. And, as touches of gray silvered their hair, their charm seemed to increase, so that in many ways they became models for others to follow. They did the right thing in the right way at the right time, no matter what the circumstances. Any social function was enhanced by the distinguished presence of Captain Beauchamp and Madeleine.

Although Madeleine made no attempt to fit into the merry, sophisticated social life, she knew she was respected and admired. Fortunately, Captain Beauchamp continued to be her friend and paid regular visits when he was in town. She suspected that he was secretly relieved that she had refused his proposal. After all, he had passed her by over twenty years ago because he loved the sea more than he loved her. Now that they were older, it seemed doubtful he would be happy with a predictable domestic life.

In the privacy of Madeleine's house, where for years Captain Beauchamp was a frequent guest, they preserved much of their public formality both in dress and behavior. Madeleine had never seen him when he was not wearing a cravat and a well-tailored coat, nor had he seen her when she was not dressed much as she would be when she stepped outside the door.

Although they observed all the necessary punctilios, which they had been trained to do, they were relaxed and easy in each other's company most of the time. Sometimes they had arguments that were almost domestic in nature: whether he should buy more property near Magnolia Grove as an investment, who would be a good husband for Solange, or what should Madeleine do about Mary Claire's future. At times they sounded, even to themselves, like husband and wife. Certainly Solange learned to depend on him as a surrogate father. Much of her love and knowledge of the river and boats were gleaned from Captain Beauchamp.

Over only one subject did he and Madeleine show strong emotion—their feelings for each other. Ever since the voyage on *les Belles Soeurs*, he had been in love with her, but it was a respectful, resigned, almost tolerant kind of love that made him available when he was needed and invisible when he was not. During the hectic years of her marriage to Jacques, he had been a barely and rarely seen presence on the horizon of her consciousness. In the years after, during her determined widowhood, when she occasionally saw Captain Beauchamp, he acted hopeful but seldom insistent, attentive but not demonstrative—or at least not very often.

They were never completely alone until, late one afternoon in 1751, he rowed her out on the Mississippi to show her his new ship, *les Belles Soeurs II*, a larger replica of the original ship that meant so much to them. He had given the watchman the night off so they could be alone. As they stood on the gently rocking deck, stirring memories in both of them, he reached out, caressed Madeleine's waist, and let his hand rest on her hip. "I like it that you still have the trimmest waist of any woman I know."

"Oh, Jean Paul," she said, moving not too rapidly out

of his reach. "Let's not have one of *those* discussions again."

"Why not? I care deeply for you and I think you like me a little. I'm a healthy man and you're a lovely woman. Why can't we enjoy a little physical contact in this life?"

She looked at him, a little wry smile on her face. "Of course, I like you. You're a fine man. But let's not spoil...."

"Spoil?" he interrupted in controlled frustration. "I don't want to spoil our relationship. I want to enhance it. Ever since the first time I saw you, I've wanted to take you in my arms and kiss you passionately, and then to undress you...."

"Please, now. No more of this." She moved hurriedly to the other side of the deck and stood with her back to him.

Beauchamp moved quickly behind her, grasped her upper arms, and gently kissed the back of her neck. She stood quite still, even as he moved his hands down her arms and encircled her waist. Easily, lightly, slowly he kissed her neck, her ears, her cheek, but she did not turn. "I love you, Madeleine," he said softly. "I have always loved you." Boldly he put his hands on her shoulders and turned her to face him; then he cupped her face tenderly in his massive hands and kissed her gently on the lips. Almost involuntarily, with just a hint of hunger, her lips softened slightly in response. She hugged him with a brief, self-conscious gesture then pushed him away.

"Jean Paul," she said, trying to move away from him, "let's return to shore. The sun is beginning to set."

"Damn it all, Madeleine, I want you."

"Well, maybe I feel the same, but we can't give in to those feelings"

"Why not? I'm yours any time you say. I've been

proposing, directly and indirectly, for years and you have put me off with one excuse or another."

"I'm used to being a widow; and, admit it, you're used to your freedom. You like sailing away whenever you want and for how long you want."

"Bullshit!" he exploded in shipboard anger.

"Please, Jean Paul, don't be vulgar. It doesn't become you."

A little chastened, but still seething in frustration, Captain Beauchamp said, "I'm sorry, Madeleine. I apologize for my language, but not for the feeling that motivated it. Well, if you won't marry me, why can't we just go to bed and...?"

Madeleine tensed. "I will not be a loose woman," she said icily. "If you want such a woman, get a little house down on Rampart Street."

"I just might do that," he replied, but with little conviction. "A nice quadroon might be stimulating." He smiled to himself and shook his head in puzzled resignation. "But no matter how good she was in bed or out, she wouldn't be you, my dear." He moved toward the ladder to their rowboat, this time to leave. "Well, consider yourself proposed to once again. And think about it, Madeleine. We have a lot of years ahead of us. Let's don't waste them."

She extended her hand for a formal *adieu* to the ship and smiled with genuine affection. "I will think about it." But the truth was Madeleine liked not being married. She loved being in complete control of her life at last. When Jacques died, she no longer feared losing her home and livelihood, so she lost much of her earlier ambition to expand. She put only enough of her land under cultivation to provide food and a modest income. She could center her life now in New Orleans, finally fulfilling her dreams of living the life of a genteel lady. She could continue her volunteer work at the school, orphanage, and hospital and remain a model of virtue and good works. Why did she need another man to tell her what she could and could not do?

Jean Paul took her extended hand to guide her back down the ladder. Perhaps at the thought of parting again, they both felt a lightning bolt shoot through the warm flesh of their hands. She stumbled in shock. He caught her by the shoulders and pulled her into his body. Madeleine started to protest, then felt the warmth of his powerful chest, his trim belly, the hardness between his legs. They felt the spark of fire up and down their bodies. He put his head on top of hers and breathed in the scent of her hair. She loosened her body and relaxed into his.

Mon Dieu, she thought, I feel as I did when the conjure woman gave me the magic potion at the waterfall and Solange was conceived. Maybe Jean Paul is a magic potion. When he kissed her this time, she opened her mouth and welcomed his tongue. When he lifted her skirt and cupped her buttocks, she rubbed the lower part of her body against him. They felt even more fire. She stunned them both by pulling down the bodice of her dress so he could caress her still firm breasts and put his mouth on her nipples. She shrieked at the sharp pleasure. He moaned.

He picked her up and half-carried her down the gangway to his dark cabin. Not taking time to light the lantern, they frantically removed their clothes, threw them on the floor, and fell onto the large bunk. He entered her moist, welcome body and the fire grew until it exploded in both of them, first in Madeleine then in Jean Paul. The burning melted into a warm liquid.

Jean Paul then lit the lantern hanging on the wall. They looked at each other and laughed in embarrassment.

Madeleine said, "What have I done? I'm as bad as Marie O'Brien or any of her whores."

"No, my darling, you have finally released a part of yourself I saw so many years ago on our voyage to New Orleans. We can make this respectable. We can marry immediately."

She shrunk away from him. "Oh, no, not a wife again!" She thought in horror about how Jacques had changed after marriage.

John Paul pulled her gently toward him and reassured her. "I will not be like Jacques—or any conventional husband. I respect you too much to change you. You can continue with your work with the Ursulines and at Magnolia Grove. And I will admit that I want to be free to go to sea now and then. We have both worked too hard to give up the lives we love, but we can enrich each other's lives."

Madeleine relaxed a little into his arms and considered his shocking proposal. She wondered if any man could keep his promise not to dominate his wife. If any man could, that man would be Jean Paul Beauchamp. "Then why get married," she asked, "if we don't change our lives?"

"To make an honest woman of you, of course," he said with a smile. "Madeleine, I know how proper and religious you are. I want to continue to make love to you and have a closer, legal bond—not a chain binding us but a symbol of our commitment. Marriage, even a quiet, quick ceremony by a priest will accomplish that."

"*Mon Dieu*, is that possible? Would we have to live together? Would we have to tell people?"

"Not if you don't want to, *ma cherie*. We can try it out

and see if it works before we announce our new situation. I will still accompany you to social events and visit you occasionally at Magnolia Grove and be the perfect gentleman. If you are comfortable with our marriage, we can have a public ceremony. But you have to promise to make special visits to my ship when we are both in New Orleans. And maybe to the cabin I'm planning to build on my land next to Magnolia Grove."

Feeling the safety of a man's arms for the first time, Madeleine considered his radical plan and cemented the deal with her eager body.

The next day Madeleine stood with Jean Paul before a priest in a small chapel and became Madeleine Boucher (de Mandeville) Bouligny Beauchamp. Their only witness was Sister Pauline. Neither the priest nor the nun was asked to lie for them but only to delay the announcement until or if they were ready to live openly as man and wife. For the first time in her life Madeleine trusted a man and relaxed her defensive walls. She felt confident that his patience and wisdom would help balance her own need to control her headstrong daughter, Solange. More important, she felt the peasant girl who arrived in New Orleans twenty-three years ago fold into the strong, independent woman she was now.

End of Book 1

STAY TUNED FOR BOOK 2!

Solange

DAUGHTER OF LAST FRENCH CASQUETTE BRIDE IN NEW ORLEANS

The daring, voluptuous Solange Bouligny de Villere Nunez Burke combines her father's sensuality and rebellion with her mother Madeleine's beauty and hard-working, practical streak. She marries three times to three different men under three different flags (French, Spanish, American) and becomes a success independently of them.

COMING SOON

About Atmosphere Press

Atmosphere Press is an independent, full-service publisher for excellent books in all genres and for all audiences. Learn more about what we do at atmospherepress.com.

We encourage you to check out some of Atmosphere's latest releases, which are available at Amazon.com and via order from your local bookstore:

The Tattered Black Book, a novel by Lexy Duck
American Genes, a novel by Kirby Nielsen
The Red Castle, a novel by Noah Verhoeff
Newer Testaments, a novel by Philip Brunetti
All Things in Time, a novel by Sue Buyer
Hobson's Mischief, a novel by Caitlin Decatur
The Black-Marketer's Daughter, a novel by Suman Mallick
The Farthing Quest, a novel by Casey Bruce
This Side of Babylon, a novel by James Stoia
Within the Gray, a novel by Jenna Ashlyn
For a Better Life, a novel by Julia Reid Galosy
Where No Man Pursueth, a novel by Micheal E. Jimerson
Here's Waldo, a novel by Nick Olson
Tales of Little Egypt, a historical novel by James Gilbert
The Hidden Life, a novel by Robert Castle
Big Beasts, a novel by Patrick Scott
Alvarado, a novel by John W. Horton III
Nothing to Get Nostalgic About, a novel by Eddie Brophy
Whose Mary Kate, a novel by Jane Leclere Doyle

About the Author

Wanda Maureen Miller (or Mo) grew up on an Arkansas farm in the 1940s and 1950s, got educated, moved to California, and taught college English. She has published six books—a historical romance, *The French* (1983); three textbooks, *Reading Faster and Understanding More*, Books 1, 2, and 3 (5 editions, 1976 to 2001); her slightly fictionalized memoir, *Last Trip Home*, (2018); and now Book 1: *Madeleine, Last French Casquette Bride in New Orleans*. Retired, she plays pickle-ball and is working on Book 2: *Solange, Daughter of Last French Casquette Bride in New Orleans*.

CPSIA information can be obtained
at www.ICGtesting.com
Printed in the USA
BVHW080810290321
603636BV00001B/31